BURIED TREASURES

OF THE

PACIFIC

NORTHWEST

Books in W. C. Jameson's *Buried Treasures* series:

BURIED TREASURES
OF THE
PACIFIC
NORTHWEST

Secret Indian Mines, Lost Outlaw Hoards,
and Stolen Payroll Coins

W. C. JAMESON

August House Publishers, Inc.
LITTLE ROCK

Published 1995 by August House, Inc.,
P.O. Box 3223, Little Rock, Arkansas, 72203,
501-372-5450.

Printed in the United States of America

10 9 8 7 6 5 4 3 2

LIBRARY OF CONGRESS CATALOGING-IN-PUBLICATION DATA

Jameson, W.C., 1942–
Buried treasures of the Pacific Northwest : secret Indian mines, lost outlaw
hoards, and stolen payroll coins / W.C. Jameson.
p .   cm.
Includes bibliographical references.

ISBN-13: 978-0-87483-438-3
ISBN-10: 0-87483-438-4

1. Northwest, Pacific—History, Local.
2. Treasure-trove—Northwest, Pacific. I. Title.
F851.J36   1995
979.5—dc20   95-35803

Project editor: Liz Parkhurst
Assistant editor: Sue T. Agnelli
Design director: Ted Parkhurst
Cover design and maps: Wendell E. Hall

AUGUST HOUSE, INC.   PUBLISHERS   LITTLE ROCK

To Liz and Ted Parkhurst,
for the opportunities and the inspiration

Contents

Washington

Selected References   *191*

Introduction

Several years ago, while visiting friends in Seattle, Washington, I attended a public lecture about the geographic region known as the Pacific Northwest of the United States, the domain of Oregon and Washington state. During the time that has passed since I heard the words of the speaker, I have forgotten most of what he said; one statement, however, has remained with me and serves to characterize much of the way I feel about this fascinating portion of North America. "The Pacific Northwest," said the speaker, "is remarkable in its variety of both physical environment and cultural influences."

Variety, indeed.

The next time I visited the region it was with the intention of undertaking research for this book. Once again, I was struck by the incredible diversity of landscapes and people I encountered along the way, throughout the thousands of miles I traveled in this special region.

As a result of my research, I discovered that the differences in the environments found in this area came about, in part, because of substantial, and sometimes violent, prehistoric geologic episodes, many of which involved the movement and crunching together of crustal places and the exploding of dozens of volcanoes. Subsequent changes in the land can be tied to even more of this kind of activity along with eons of continuous erosion.

The Pacific Northwest is also home to an impressive richness and variety of cultures. American Indians,

Russians, Swedes, the French and British, and many generations of Americans have found their way into this region, lured largely by the abundant resources and the opportunities they offered. Surely, the eclectic mix of humankind found here would be hard to replicate anywhere else in the world.[*]

This exciting and fertile combination of diversity in land and people can and has yielded many cultural fruits, and foremost among them is an incredible array of folklore pertinent to the region of the Pacific Northwest. From the time of the early Indian occupants, traders, and trappers through the boom times of mineral excavation to the present day, the Pacific Northwest has been a rich source of American folklore, legend, and tales, particularly those that relate to lost mines and buried treasures.

Origins

The often rugged and generally picturesque physical settings found in the Pacific Northwest—regardless of whether one is considering the coastline, the tall, snow-capped peaks, the interior deserts, or the eastern plateau—are products of numerous sequences of eons-old geologic events.

Millions of years ago, the leading edge of the westward-drifting North American crustal plate pushed against the trailing edge of the slower-moving Pacific plate. The

---

[*] While the Pacific Northwest has enjoyed the substantial cultural contributions of Asian and Polynesian immigrants, the folklore surrounding lost treasures in this region does not reflect this. Since many Chinese immigrants of the mid-nineteenth century worked as indentured servants, they had little opportunity to seek wealth or treasure. During the California Gold Rush, the Chinese were only allowed to work played-out mines, which the *Dictionary of the American West* (New York: Facts on File, 1993) cites as the occasion for the phrase "a Chinaman's chance."

movements of these extensive rock platforms, governed by powerful currents of molten magma found miles below the surface, had a dramatic impact on the environments of the region, then and now. The compressional stress exerted by the two plates proceeded at an incredibly slow rate—mere millimeters per year. The consistent pressure over time, however, forced the breaking and buckling of much of this section of the North American crust such that great portions of it were bent, folded, buckled, and elevated to altitudes measured in thousands of feet. As the crust was weakened from this prolonged impact and compression, pressurized magma, the molten rock from deep below the crust, surged through faults, exploding to the surface and heaving millions of tons of ash into the atmosphere, spreading dozens of square miles of lava across the landscape, and resulting in the formation of tall volcanic peaks such as Mount Adams, Mount St. Helens, Mount Hood, and Mount Ranier.

After the passage of several million more years, these episodes yielded to relatively quieter times, but the north-south trending mountains thus formed—ranging from the coast to over one hundred miles inland—began to exert a profound impact on the leeward lands to the east.

The normal path of weather patterns, which originated hundreds of miles away in the Pacific Ocean and traveled in an easterly to southeasterly direction onto the continent, were now disrupted by the significant topographic obstacle presented by this young crest of mountains. The humid air, resulting from contact with the ocean waters, was forced upward by the mountain barrier. As it rose to high altitudes it cooled, resulting in the condensation of the water vapor. Clouds formed, droplets merged and grew heavy, and fell out as rain along the windward slope of the mountains. To this day, rainfall on some windward portions of these mountains reaches a hundred inches per year.

From the leeward foothills to approximately one hundred miles to the east, the lands that depended on this moisture for the sustenance of the forests were now deprived of customary rainfall. Years progressed into centuries, and soon great portions of the vast interior grew dry and eventually evolved into desert and steppe environments.

East of these dry lands, the higher elevations of yet another tectonically formed plateau provided drainage for great rivers and streams emanating from glacier- and snow-topped elevations. During subsequent millenia, these streams cut through the rock and led to the formation of impressive canyons and gorges. Gradually these lands produced environments, resources, and characteristics that appealed to the newcomers moving into the region with an eye toward settlement.

The coastal areas, long a favored habitation for American Indians, provided fish and shellfish for sustenance and the furs of otters and sea lions for clothing and trade. In later years, portions of the coastline would be claimed by seagoing explorers and traders as ports and harbors to accommodate the great sailing vessels transporting goods and passengers.

In mountains and foothills, a cloak of flora and fauna evolved, eventually yielding resources of timber and wildlife—timber that would become the backbone of the forest products industry and wild game that was easily and often harvested by the newcomers. Here and there in the rock that was so dramatically influenced by the surging magma of prehistory, gold and other precious minerals thus formed awaited harvest, for centuries of erosion by glaciers and flowing water gradually removed the covering layers of rock and exposed veins of rich mineral.

Between the foothills and the more arid portions of the intermontane basins could be found fertile, arable land containing deep, nutritious soils reaching thicknesses of several feet and providing a setting for much of the agricultural potential that would come to be realized throughout this area.

The highlands of the east, called the Columbia–Snake River Plateau, are characterized by vast areas of level terrain formed by massive lava flows from the prehistoric past along with scattered hills and mountains and deep, river-cut canyons. Many of these rivers flowed toward the Pacific Ocean, sometimes serving as barriers to cross, other times providing water for thirsty travelers and crops.

Variety? To be sure. And an array of land and resources that held appeal for a great variety of people who would eventually make their homes here.

Culture

The Pacific Northwest has long been a favored location for exploration, settlement, prospecting, and resource acquisition for many different kinds of people, and the flux of various ethnic groups into and through this region has added to the mix and diversity of cultures, both historically and presently. The first humans to claim the Pacific Northwest as their home were various tribes of American Indians including the Salish, the Chinook, and the Yurok. Here in this vital corner of what was eventually to become an important part of the United States, these descendants of Asian migrants who crossed the Bering land bridge generations earlier found the necessary elements for survival— water, food, and shelter. Fish were plentiful in the streams and rivers, and game was abundant nearly everywhere. Seacoast dwellers reaped the bounty of fish and shellfish from the coastal waters while inland tribes harvested elk, deer, moose, bear, a variety of game birds, and other animals from the bountiful forests. And from the numerous rock outcrops in the mountains, many of the tribes extracted gold and silver for use in fashioning ornaments.

Indians did not remain the only occupants of this land for long, for research has uncovered abundant evidence of centuries-old Spanish exploration, settlement, and mining in the Pacific Northwest. In the late sixteenth century and much of the seventeenth century, the Spanish, in their quest for knowledge about and riches in the new world, made several attempts at mining in this region, many of which were apparently successful. Following the departure of the Spaniards from this region, Mexicans occasionally made the long journey up from their homeland far to the south to continue the mining activities, both in the old Spanish mines and with new excavation. Mexican gold miners were found in the area as recently as the mid-1800s.

Seagoing vessels from Europe eventually brought explorers and traders to the shores of the Pacific Northwest. On many occasions, ships were anchored in calm bays while sailors rowed to the nearby shore to assess the resources of the region. And for years, boats carrying booty— in the form of gold, silver, and jewelry looted from Indian civilizations far to the south—and trading ships that plied the waters of the Pacific stopped here to bury their wealth on the remote beaches. Pirate ships were rumored to have left chests filled with stolen ingots and other treasures hidden in secluded locations along the coast of the Pacific Northwest. Only a few ever returned to reclaim their caches.

Early fur trappers and explorers of French and English descent were among the first white men to visit the mountains and other inland portions of the Pacific Northwest and remain for any significant length of time. While an occasional discovery of precious metal was reported, these adventurous souls were primarily interested in another kind of wealth. The fur of the beaver and other animals was harvested in great quantities from the area rivers and streams, fur that served as raw material for the manufacturing of hats and coats to cover monied residents in the east and across the sea in Europe. Reports of the abundance of beaver and other fur-bearing animals brought even more trappers and explorers into the region, many of whom settled here after taking Indian wives.

Russian seamen also discovered possibilities related to the fur trade. Initially, Russian seagoing vessels sailed these coastal waters during the process of hunting and securing fur from seals, sea lions, and otters. Encouraged by this success, some early coastal settlements evolved, and for a number of years, trade between Russians, Europeans, and Indians was brisk.

As fantastic reports of the abundance of resources—not only furs, but forests, arable land, and minerals—began to filter eastward into the more populous regions of the United States, many who dreamed of owning land and exploring new territories were drawn to the Pacific Northwest. Potential settlers, businessmen, speculators, and many who simply desired a change of environment or a chance to make a new start traveled the long distances to Washington and Oregon to view the land for themselves. Sometimes great wagon trains arrived in the region, carrying dozens of men, women, and children intent on coaxing crops out of the fertile ground, planting orchards, and establishing thriving communities with schools and churches. At first they trickled into the territory in relatively small numbers, but as time passed, they began arriving by the thousands.

And they are still coming.

In 1848, gold was discovered at Sutter's Mill in California, an event that inspired the westward migration of tens of thousands of eager gold-seekers over the next several years, the so-called Forty-Niners. Young and old, they migrated from the farms and the towns of the East, South, and Midwest across the largely unsettled continent into California in search of their fortunes. To them, California, now called the Golden State, represented their promised land, the place where they could fulfill their dreams.

Some few did achieve wealth, but more often than not most of the gold hunters failed in their quest and returned home. Many, however, decided to journey into the relatively unpopulated Pacific Northwest environs of Oregon and Washington to continue their prospecting and mining activities, questing for gold and other precious metals in the heretofore neglected mountains and foothills of the Coast and Cascade Ranges. There, uncluttered by the dense clusters of prospectors and miners that had earlier descended upon the mountains of California, the gold-seekers in Oregon and Washington encountered large tracts of unclaimed land and prospects, regions that ultimately provided bountiful yields of gold and other minerals, mineral wealth taken from the rock by the patient, hard-working, and fortunate few who ventured into the region.

The impressive and oft-reported successes associated with the Pacific Northwest mines lured another element—the outlaw. Many a miner was killed for his poke, and many a shipment of high-grade ore being escorted from mine to smelter was stolen by roving bands of badmen. Fortunes in gold ingots, coins, and nuggets were purloined and often cached. Many of the robbers were either killed or captured before they could recover and spend their hidden wealth, and those treasures remain lost to this day.

Lost Mines and Buried Treasures of the Pacific Northwest

The diversity of immigrants, coupled with the numerous and manifold motivations that brought them into the Pacific Northwest, gradually resulted in a fertile mixture of residents. Each group, ethnic and racial, carried into this region as part of its cultural baggage important elements of its respective civilizations—foodways, religion, language, dress, architecture, music, and, of course, folk legends.

Among the immigrant cultures, systems of trade evolved. Not just the trade of goods and supplies, but a sharing of other cultural bounties, including the stories, both those imported into the region and others generated from within the environment. Soon there materialized in the society fascinating and often spellbinding tales of great

16

discoveries of gold, of fortunes found and lost, of pirate treasure, of lost mines, of buried riches.

One of the earliest writers to research and publish these captivating tales was Ruby El Hult. In 1957, she published *Lost Mines and Treasures of the Pacific Northwest,* which was followed in 1971 with *Treasure Hunting Northwest.* Any research or investigation into tales of lost mines and buried treasures in the Pacific Northwest must begin with Hult's collections. But like the discovery of a single tiny gold nugget in the bed of a clear stream, Hult's writings invited even more search and research. Employing information and leads gleaned from Hult's writings, I spent hundreds of hours in libraries and collections throughout the region in search of documents, journals, newspaper reports, books, and articles, all relating to tales of lost treasure. The wealth of information grew, eventually filling entire file cabinets with long-forgotten information on the tales, the people involved, and the settings.

Hult's books carried names of individuals who, years earlier, were involved in searches for lost mines and buried treasures. Some of them actually discovered hidden caches or covered-over mine shafts. A few of them were still living when I undertook the initial research for this book, and, often with great difficulty, I was able to locate and interview them. In addition, I also contacted and interviewed many contemporary treasure hunters and researchers. The collective experiences of the young and old gold seekers contributed important insight and knowledge, much of which I hope I have captured in many of the tales presented in this book.

Furthermore, I made extensive expeditions in search of many of the lost mines and buried treasures described herein. For hundreds of miles, I, along with others, packed across remote portions of mountain ranges, followed sinuous canyons from mouth to source, hiked miles of coastline, entered long-abandoned mine shafts, and dug for treasure and history in the earth and sands of the region.

We visited and explored places I believed existed only in the minds of men.

Did we find treasure? Did we encounter any lost mines? Did we dig up a cache of gold ingots? As any professional treasure hunter knows, the announcement of important discoveries is discouraged for a number of reasons, not the least of which is to protect the property on which the treasure has been found. Suffice it to say we returned from our expedition wealthier than when we arrived, and much of that wealth was related to the knowledge we gained, the information we acquired. We returned with evidence that most, if not all, of the stories contained in this book, though regarded by some as fanciful, are in all probability true. The stories included here are those that held up under sometimes exhaustive research and correlation with known historical events. Several tales that were particularly appealing had to be left out of the book simply because there was no evidence of their validity.

There is something magical about tales of lost mines and buried treasures, something that exerts a strong appeal on most people. Many of us, whether we admit it or not, harbor a longing for wealth. We all hope to win a lottery. We wait patiently for an announcement we have won a sweepstakes. We often dream of finding a lost mine or a buried treasure.

The Pacific Northwest is rich in such tales. In the following pages, many of these stories are presented. Many of the treasures and mines described herein actually existed, and in fact exist to this day. Many await the patient and fortunate treasure hunter who may someday stumble upon a fabulously wealthy cache or long-lost gold mine.

But perhaps more importantly, these tales represent a cultural artifact from that eclectic mix of people that moved into and settled the region formally known as the Pacific Northwest.

These treasures are real. People continue to hunt for them even today, and once in a while one or another of them is actually found. The stories, though about actual treasure, represent a kind of cultural treasure too—they are a product of the people who made the Pacific Northwest what it is today.

Like photographs and books of decades past, these stories provide insight into a fascinating world of wealth, adventure, mystery, and hope.

OREGON

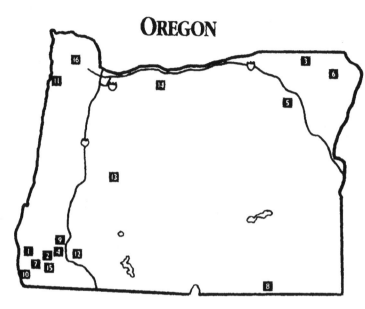

1. Private Manley Martin's Gold Ledge

2. Karl Meyer's Mysterious Lost Cave of Gold

3. Lost Gold of Devil's Sink
   Fortune in Stolen Loot Hidden in Devil's Sink

4. Sterling Creek Valley Lode

5. Lost Saddlebags of Gold Coins

6. The Nez Perce Gold

7. The Lost Ramsey Party Gold

8. Lost Blue Bucket Gold

9. Ed Schieffelin's Lost Lode

10. The Curious Sir Francis Drake Treasure

11. Buried Pirate Treasure on Oregon Shore

12. Mount Mazama Gold

13. The Lost Log Cabin Placer

14. The Lost Hermit Treasure

15. Deathbed Confession Discloses Cache of Gold

16. Secret Gold Mine of the Chinook Indians

Private Manley Martin's
Gold Ledge

Manley Martin joined the army at seventeen years of age in his home state of Kentucky in the year 1852. Long had the youth dreamed of becoming a soldier and leading campaigns into rugged and unknown portions of the West, into and beyond the Rocky Mountains, of which he had heard so many tantalizing tales. Donning the uniform of the Army of the United States, Martin anticipated fulfilling his dream.

After enlisting, Martin learned that the First Dragoons were to be sent to western Oregon to defend settlers from rampaging Indians. At the first opportunity, he volunteered for the unit and soon found himself, the youngest Dragoon, heading west.

Shortly after arriving, the Dragoons were stationed at Port Orford, a coastal village located in southwestern Oregon overlooking the Pacific Ocean. After being consigned to the little settlement for several weeks, Martin grew extremely bored and was beginning to second-guess his decision to become a Dragoon. Within a few days, however, Dragoon leader Lt. Stoneman went about the military encampment asking for volunteers to go with him into the nearby Coquille Mountains. Martin was the first to offer his services.

Led by Stoneman, Private Martin, along with Sergeant Mann and Privates McKenna, Ross, Schlisk, and Schnedicker, rode into the Coquilles, a division of the Coast Range. Leading packhorses loaded with gear and supplies, the small party planned to be away from camp for about three weeks.

Instead of fighting Indians, Martin was disappointed to learn that this expedition had been sent out to survey and determine the best route for a road from Port Orford to Jacksonville, a booming community some eighty miles as the crow flies to the southeast.

After nearly three weeks of riding and surveying, the Dragoon contingent completed their task and, though nearly out of food, undertook the long return trip to Port Orford. On reentering a portion of the Coquille Mountains near the Rogue River, a heavy rainstorm struck the area, washing out trails and generating numerous mud slides. Stoneman soon found himself hopelessly lost and confused. Deciding the best thing to do would be to make camp for the evening and consult his maps, the lieutenant selected a suitable clearing and ordered the men to set up camp and start dinner.

Tired and hungry, the soldiers were eager for the break and, though weary from the long day's ride, approached their assignments with enthusiasm. As Ross and McKenna collected what little dry wood could be found in the area and got a fire going, Schlisk and Schnedicker set up the tents. Martin, carrying two buckets, walked down a nearby incline to obtain water from the creek that trickled along the bottom.

As Martin filled the buckets, the clouds parted and late-afternoon sunshine filtered through the forest canopy. Rising to return to the campsite, the private spotted a reflection of light from a rock ledge a few feet away and across the little creek. Looking closer, he discerned a smattering of yellowish glint lacing through a layer of white quartz. Using his saber, Martin carefully pried out a chunk of the rock and placed it in his pocket.

On returning to camp, Martin decided to have some fun with his companions. After setting down the water buckets, he pulled the piece of quartz from his pocket and tossed it onto the ground near the campfire, telling his fellow soldiers he had discovered gold. In truth, Martin had never seen gold before in his life.

Sergeant Mann, prior to joining the army, had prospected and panned for gold in the mountains far to the south in California. He picked up the piece of quartz, and, after inspecting it for a moment, turned to Martin and told him it did, in fact, contain gold. Furthermore, insisted Mann, the gold was quite pure and abundant.

On hearing the sergeant's words, the rest of the soldiers, including Stoneman, grew excited and rushed down to the creek. After Martin pointed out the ledge where he found the gold, all of the men pried pieces of the ore-filled quartz loose with sabers and knives, filling their pockets and pouches.

That evening around the camp, the soldiers talked about the gold and about returning for it after completing their military service. They spoke of becoming wealthy and of the things they would purchase. That night, they slept well, their heads filled with dreams of the future.

The following morning brought cold weather and very little food for breakfast. After breaking camp and loading the packhorses, the Dragoons rode out in the hope of finding some recognizable landmark. Before leaving, however, Stoneman suggested they cut some marks on the trees in order to identify the campsite, thereby making it easier to relocate on a return trip. Four trees were blazed, each one forming a corner of a large square. In the exposed wood, each of the soldiers carved his name.

After surviving for three more days solely on the wild game they shot, the soldiers finally returned to Port Orford. At the camp, their conversations remained filled with talk of gold and riches, but as time passed the fervor lessened. It would be at least a full year before any of them could be released from the army, and the thought of reentering the mountains filled with hostile Indians was often discouraging.

Though initially enthusiastic about the gold discovery, Stoneman lost interest quickly. His lifelong goal was to be a career military officer, and he oriented his energies in that direction. In time, Stoneman earned the rank of general. After leaving the army years later, he entered politics and was eventually elected governor of California.

Privates Schlisk and Schnedicker were the first to be released from military service, and on mustering out, the first thing they did was make preparations to return to the location of the gold ledge and dig the ore. Traveling to Jacksonville, they organized a company of about a dozen men and attempted to retrace the route followed by Stoneman the previous year. For weeks they combed the mountains in the region of Jump-Off Joe Creek and Graves Creek, but they never found anything.

A short time later, Martin, after being honorably discharged by the army, entered the Coquille Mountains in search of the ledge, but came away unsuccessful and discouraged when he was unable to locate the campsite.

Meanwhile, Captain William H. Packwood was placed in command of the First Dragoons and learned of the gold discovery from Private McKenna, a member of Stoneman's party. Intrigued with the tale, Packwood recorded several pages of notes pertaining to directions and details as they were provided by the enlisted man. From the description, Packwood was convinced he could locate the gold-filled ledge.

When Packwood was finally discharged from his military obligation, he and a friend named George Abbott went into partnership in a cattle ranch and some mining interests. All the while, Packwood maintained a deep interest in the gold he believed existed somewhere in the Coquille

Mountains. He began to refer to it as Martin's Gold, after the young soldier who discovered it.

Packwood learned of the search undertaken by Schlisk and Schnedicker as well as that of Martin. He made notes about the areas searched by the men, and added this information to his growing store of knowledge about the gold ledge. But for years he remained busy with his ranching and mining interests and, burdened with these responsibilities, found it difficult to undertake an expedition into the Coquille Mountains in search of the gold. In 1861, he moved to Enchanted Prairie, where he met and made friends with several prospectors.

While visiting with his new companions one evening, Packwood heard an amazing story. Several weeks earlier, the prospectors had been ranging in the Coquille Mountains in an area bisected by Cow Creek when they came upon a clearing. Four large oak trees, each of which accounted for a corner of a rough square near the edges of the clearing, bore blaze marks into which were inscribed names. The prospectors had unknowingly located Stoneman's camp! Aware that Martin's gold ledge was nearby, Packwood pressed his friends for more details.

Teaming up with a new friend named Collins, Packwood organized an expedition into the mountains. After several days of riding and searching, the two men found the campsite and the four marked trees. One of the trees had blown down, but the other three were clearly marked and the names of the soldiers could still be read in the exposed wood.

For the next several days, Packwood and Collins ranged throughout the region searching for the creek where Martin obtained water and which flowed past the gold ledge. Oddly, no creek was to be found anywhere within miles of the campsite. Discouraged, Packwood and Collins returned to Enchanted Prairie.

During the summer of the same year, Packwood received a surprise visitor in the person of Manley Martin!

Martin, on hearing about Packwood's expedition to the Coquilles in search of the gold, decided to track the former officer down and discuss the matter with him.

Packwood related the details of his frustrating search for the golden ledge to Martin, pointing out that he had found the campsite but no gold, not even a creek.

To this Martin only laughed. He told Packwood that the creek only ran during and shortly after a rainstorm; otherwise, it was completely dry. To Packwood's surprise, Martin told him that the ledge containing the gold was nowhere near the blazed trees!

Martin then made Packwood an offer. If the ex-captain would lead him to the old campsite, Martin would show Packwood the location of the ledge. The two men shook hands and agreed to depart in a few days.

The next morning, Packwood was paid a social visit by a man who owned a neighboring ranch. As the two men spoke, Packwood mentioned the existence of the gold-filled ledge in the Coquille Mountains and his intention to travel into the region to find the ore. Fascinated by this story, the neighbor, a man named Brown, begged to be allowed to accompany Packwood and Martin. In a weak moment, Packwood consented.

When Martin arrived a few days later, leading a pack-horse loaded with gear, he became furious when he learned Packwood had invited a third party to accompany them.

To make matters worse, Brown was a vocal supporter of the Union and, as the Civil War was underway, loudly and continuously denigrated the Confederacy and its policies. Martin, who sided strongly with the South, took exception and the two men argued bitterly for several days as they rode into the mountains.

Packwood, Martin, and Brown eventually arrived at the old campsite with little difficulty and, in a short time, located the three remaining blazed trees. After setting up a simple camp, Martin, who said he wished to walk around a bit to get his bearings, disappeared into the forest. Martin remained away from camp for hours and returned well after dark to find Packwood and Brown already asleep.

The following morning, Martin announced to his two traveling companions that he was leaving, and after packing his gear, rode away toward the Rogue River.

Packwood was angered and disappointed, but there was not much he could do. Brown suspected Martin had actually relocated the golden ledge and simply did not want to share the information with the others.

On a hunch, Packwood and Brown tried to follow Martin's trail from the previous day. For nearly four miles, they retraced his route, following bent grass, broken branches, and footprints in the moist soil. Eventually, they came to a tiny stream, actually an ephemeral tributary to Cow Creek. Not far from this little stream, they were surprised to find another blazed tree. At this point, however, they lost Martin's trail and, though they searched for hours, were unable to pick it up again. Experiencing failure once again in his quest to find the gold, Packwood could do little else but return home.

About two months after his latest expedition into the Coquille Mountains, Packwood received a letter from Martin. In the missive, the former soldier confessed he had gone to the gold-filled ledge on the afternoon he left Packwood and Brown in camp. Martin admitted he didn't wish to share any of the gold with the boorish Union sympathizer.

Packwood was still determined to find the ledge and began to make plans to organize yet a third expedition into the mountains. As he was engaged in this project, Packwood learned of the discovery of gold in eastern Oregon near the Washington state line, so he decided to try his luck there. As the years passed and Packwood experienced success in other mining endeavors, as well as in ranching and real estate, he gradually lost his desire to return to the Coquille Mountains.

In 1914, when Packwood was an elderly man—in his nineties—he accompanied a National Forest Service ranger into the Coquilles. Out of curiosity, he wanted to see if he could relocate the old Stoneman campsite. When Packwood and the ranger arrived in the general area of the camp, the old man saw that a forest fire had consumed much of the tree growth, causing some confusion relative to certain landmarks. This was Packwood's last trip into the mountains. When he returned home he considered mounting yet another expedition to try to find the gold ledge. It was not to happen. Old age and serious health problems had taken a toll on Packwood, so he contented himself with wondering about what might have been had he ever found Martin's gold.

The blazed trees are gone, and the little creek that runs just below the ledge of gold is normally dry. A few people who know the story of Private Manley Martin's lost ledge of gold have entered the region from time to time in search of it, but it has always eluded them.

Virtually untouched, the location of this gold deposit has remained a mystery for more than 140 years.

Karl Meyer's Mysterious Lost Cave of Gold

Karl Meyer arrived on American shores sometime during the early 1800s with many of the same ambitions and desires as thousands of other immigrants. A native German, Meyer sought more and greater opportunities here than were available to him in his homeland—opportunities that, he hoped fervently, would bring him wealth, prestige, and a life of luxury. Eagerly, Karl Meyer anticipated his new citizenship status, and he was determined to become an important man in this young country.

Even though Meyer wanted many of the same things as the other immigrants, he remained, in many ways, quite different from them, too. Instead of living near the edge of poverty and having few skills, Meyer possessed a degree in geology from the University of Berlin. Though he worked as a mineralogist for a time in Germany, he cared little for working for others. Karl Meyer wanted to become a miner, to be sure, but more than that, he wanted to become a mining entrepreneur. Opportunities for such were limited in his native Germany, so, having a firm notion of what he wished to accomplish, he departed for the United States where he knew greater opportunities for success existed.

Meyer resided for several months in Pittsburgh, Pennsylvania, where he worked as a clerk in a dry goods store. After he had saved enough money to purchase some supplies, a good riding horse, and a sturdy mule, he set off on a long journey west. Specifically, Meyer decided to travel to Oregon and try his luck prospecting around the Klamath Mountains in the southwestern part of the state.

The spring of 1878 found Meyer guiding his horse and mule along a narrow, rocky trail that paralleled Miller Creek in the Klamaths. As he slowly followed the contours of the land, he scanned the nearby rock outcrops with his trained eye, constantly searching for any promise of minerals. At one point during his ride, Meyer passed a dense clump of huckleberry bushes, which caught the attention of his mule. It was only after several minutes of tugging on the lead rope that he was able to pull the animal away from the luscious ripe berries and continue on his journey.

Late afternoon found Meyer several miles farther up the river and setting up camp for the night while preparing a light dinner. As he consumed his meal, the German watched his animals grazing on the rich grasses that grew along the riverbank several yards away.

That night, a storm struck the area, and Meyer was awakened by booming thunder and great crackling strikes of lightning. Worried about his animals, he peered into the stormy darkness from the flap door of his leaky tent and, during the sudden and brief illumination of the landscape by a flash of lightning, discovered that the mule was gone. Believing the animal had been frightened away by the storm, and determined to locate it before the tracks were completely washed away, Meyer donned his slicker and boots and followed the mule's tracks back down the trail that paralleled the stream. As he walked in the muddy tracks, Meyer concluded the animal had merely returned to the huckleberry bushes they passed the day before.

Before he could find the mule, Meyer was forced to seek shelter from the storm, which was growing more intense by the minute. Looking about, he spied a wide niche several yards above him at the apex of a granite talus slope next to the trail. Believing the niche offered a relatively dry refuge from the driving rain, he climbed the crumbly slope and entered it. Sitting just inside the opening, Meyer quietly waited for the rains to abate before continuing his search.

Examining the rock crevice in which he sat, Meyer decided the rift had been formed by an ancient earthquake, which had split the intrusive volcanic rock that dominated this landscape.

Meyer was startled from his thoughts by the presence of a bobcat, which suddenly appeared only a few feet away at the lip of the opening. The bobcat, equally startled, quickly bounded past Meyer and deep into the dark recess of the cave. Curious as to how far this crack in the rock extended, Meyer fashioned a crude torch from the dry grasses he found just inside the opening and crawled deeper into the cave, following the tracks of the cat.

The German had crawled no more than fifty feet when the light from his torch revealed a vein of quartz bisecting one wall of the cave. Within the quartz matrix, Meyer was startled to find a thick lacing of gold! Using his knife, he pried some of the ore from the quartz and placed it into his hat.

By the time Meyer had filled the hat with gold, the rain had stopped. Hoisting the heavy hatful of gold, he carried it down to Miller Creek where he washed it off, further separating the ore from the rock.

Excited, Meyer could think of nothing except locating his mule, riding into the nearest town to replenish his supplies, and returning to mine the gold from the rich vein. Without thinking to note any pertinent landmarks, the German set out in search of his mule.

As Meyer suspected he would, he found the animal happily munching huckleberries a short distance down the trail. After leading the mule back to camp, Meyer packed his gear and set out for Grants Pass, a small mining community on the banks of the Rogue River, about fifteen miles away.

Meyer dropped his hatful of gold off at the assay office while he purchased supplies at the local mercantile. When he returned, he was stunned to discover the hatful of gold he brought in was worth an amazing $5,000! Truly, Meyer thought, he had found some of the purest gold in the entire state of Oregon. After spending the night in town, the German departed at dawn, eager to return to the isolated, gold-filled niche in the granite wall next to Miller Creek.

Late in the day, after selecting a suitable campsite near what he thought to be the location of the crevice, Meyer erected his tent and prepared dinner. Too excited to eat much, the German tossed half of his food away and walked down to the creek to clean his skillet. After washing and rinsing, Meyer rose to return to the camp when his boot slipped on a slick rock, causing the miner to fall to the ground where he cracked his head severely on the hard-packed ground.

Meyer lay unconscious for most of the night, waking about an hour before dawn. Dazed and confused, the German stumbled around his campsite, holding his aching head with both hands.

All day long Meyer remained close to camp. His head hurt badly, and he was sick to his stomach. Vaguely, he remembered something about a location where gold could be extracted from a quartz vein, but he could not sort out the confusing thoughts.

The next day, Meyer mounted his horse and rode up and down the valley of Miller Creek, hoping to recall what he was there for. At least twice, he passed just below the niche located at the top of the talus slope on the adjacent wall, the cave that contained a great fortune in gold only a few dozen feet within. Discouraged at not remembering anything, Meyer returned to his camp.

The next morning, the German decided to ride back into Grants Pass and seek medical treatment. When he arrived, he found the town alive with gossip concerning the gold he had brought a few days earlier. He eventually located a physician who examined the bump on his head and told him he had a severe concussion and a case of amnesia. Meyer returned to his camp in the hope that proximity to his barely remembered gold strike might be helpful.

For weeks, Meyer ranged up and down Miller Creek, trying in vain to sort out the jumbled recollections of finding gold in the area, but nothing helped. He constructed a crude log cabin in which to live during the coming winter months, and for the next three years he continued to search the valley for some sign of his rich gold strike.

He never relocated it.

During his third winter in the valley, Meyer contracted tuberculosis, and in the interest of his health abandoned the region and moved to a warmer, drier location in southern California. Eventually, he was confined to a rest home, where he passed away peacefully in his sleep several years later, never realizing his dream of becoming wealthy and important.

Many miners and prospectors living in the Grants Pass area traveled to the Miller Creek Valley in search of Karl Meyer's lost gold. They believed that the hatful of ore the German carried into town that day could only have come from this region, for that was the only place Meyer was known to have visited while prospecting for minerals in the Klamath Mountains. Though the area was searched for months, no one ever located the elusive cave containing the gold-filled quartz.

One observer noted that the heavy rains that struck the Miller Creek area one year caused a number of landslides and rock slides. It is believed by some that the mysterious cave discovered by Meyer might have been easily covered up by such a slide, thus sealing off access to the incredible fortune of gold lying just within.

Perhaps a future storm may someday uncover the elusive rock niche.

Lost Gold of Devil's Sink

In northeastern Oregon, deep in the northern reaches of the Blue Mountains not far from the Spout Springs Ski Area, is a strange and fascinating place called Devil's Sink. Devil's Sink is located in a region that has been topographically modified by ancient volcanic activity, and evidence of long-past lava flows and extrusive formations are common. Cracks and crevices in the basaltic crust can be found, and sinks, or collapsed areas, have given the region its name. The part of this region called Devil's Sink actually includes two collapsed sections known as the Big Sink and the Little Sink.

This extremely rugged landscape has long been considered haunted by the Indians who once resided here, populated by spirits who remain friendly only to the Indians themselves, and not always even then. Many are the tales of mysterious deaths of intruders who entered the region of Devil's Sink, and of the haunted spirits that supposedly guard the area. To this day, hikers continue to get lost in the Devil's Sink region.

The Devil's Sink, which has always been associated with strange occurrences, is also presumed by many to be the location of a rich deposit of gold, gold that has occasionally been mined in small quantities by the Indians but that has eluded searchers for at least a century. While geologists who have examined the Devil's Sink area have concluded that the presence of gold is a distinct possibility, no significant quantities have ever been discovered and mined, at least not by white men.

But it is well known among residents of northeastern Oregon that the Indians knew the location of the gold and, according to some, used it to purchase goods from time to time. Even today, many claim that a few Indians that still live in the area know exactly where the lost gold of the sinks lies, but none are talking.

Early travelers through this area carried tales to their westward destinations of local Indians bartering gold with them. Occasionally, when some of the wagon trains stopped to rest men and animals and replenish provisions at the tiny community of Elgin, some twenty miles south of Devil's Sink, the Indians would offer the migrants nuggets of almost pure gold for the bolts of colorful cloth they carried with them. Sometimes, according to journals kept during that time, the Indians would bring forth fists full of gold nuggets, apparently freshly cut from a quartz matrix, and offer to trade them for just a few feet of calico.

Invariably, some of the travelers would ask the Indians where the gold came from, but, almost fearfully, they would decline to tell them, stating that the location of the gold was filled with evil spirits that would claim the lives of any whites that dared to enter.

Years later, when Elgin grew into a prosperous town containing several businesses, the Indians would continue to arrive at the town to trade at the mercantile. In every case, they would pay for their goods with gold nuggets they claimed came from somewhere near Devil's Sink.

By the 1880s, all but a few of the Indians had disappeared. One commonly accepted tale relates that for years the Indian encampment was located just below a natural dam that held the water in the Little Sink. As a result of an earthquake, the dam ruptured, and the ensuing flood wiped out most of the tribe. Only a few of the old men remained alive.

One of the survivors, a gnarled, bent Indian in his seventies named Garquash, arrived in Elgin one morning in 1908 to purchase some food. As was his custom, he paid his bill with gold nuggets he said he dug from a shallow cave near Devil's Sink. When Garquash limped away from the town and back into the nearby mountains, three men who were quietly hanging around the mercantile decided to follow him to see if he would inadvertently lead them to the gold. For several miles they tracked the old Indian along the trail that led to Devil's Sink, but, eventually they lost him. On several other occasions they tried to follow Garquash, but the wily old Indian continued to elude them.

Sometime during the last decade of the nineteenth century, railroad tracks were being laid between the towns of Elgin and Wallowa, some twenty miles to the east as the crow flies. Many of the jobs that could be had during this time were associated with the manufacture of railroad ties. Timber cutters and sawmill operators were in great demand, and one young man who lived with his family in a remote canyon in the Blue Mountains found work at the sawmill near where Lookingglass Creek and Mottet Creek joined not far from Devil's Sink.

One weekend, the young sawmill worker decided to search for a shortcut to his home by traveling through the Devil's Sink area. In a very short time, the fellow became lost in the strange and rugged country and wandered around until nightfall, when he decided to crawl into a recessed area in a canyon wall to await daybreak. He laid down atop a bed of crumbly quartz and tried to get some sleep.

Awakening at dawn, the young man noticed the recess in which he found shelter contained a ledge of quartz. On closer inspection, he discovered the quartz was filled with gold. Looking about the small cave in which he spent the night, he concluded that the pieces of quartz on which he slept were what was left when someone mined small amounts of gold from the formation.

The sawmill operator extracted several pieces of gold from the quartz and placed them in his pockets. Following this, he continued to try to find a way out of the canyon.

That evening, he finally arrived home and showed his family the gold. He decided to resign from his sawmill job and return to the quartz ledge to mine the gold. He told his family they would be rich in a very short time.

The next day, as the young man arranged some gear for his return trip to Devil's Sink, he fell and suffered a serious break in his pelvis. For several months, he remained confined to bed, and when he was finally able to move about on his own, he found he was severely crippled, unable to take more than a few halting steps at a time before collapsing in painful agony. His dream of returning to Devil's Sink to retrieve the rich gold he found there was squashed.

Though he tried to provide directions to the gold-filled quartz ledge, repeated searches in the area by his family members were never successful.

Today, the tales of lost gold in the Devil's Sink region are well known among many eastern Oregon residents. Though no discovery of the Devil's Sink gold has been made, the search continues.

Fortune in Stolen Loot
Hidden in Devil's Sink

Devil's Sink in northeastern Oregon is associated not only with an apparently rich vein of gold ore for which people have searched for decades, it is also the location of $60,000 in gold coins taken during the holdup of a freight wagon.

The location of this hidden treasure has been known for well over a century. The problem lies in retrieving it, for evidence indicates the gold was dropped into one of the sinkholes located in the Devil's Sink region, an allegedly bottomless watery pit called Big Sink.

Around 1850, there was a lot of movement along a series of trails that linked Boise, Idaho, with the newly opened goldfields in eastern Washington. One trail in particular wound from Boise through the hills and forests of eastern Oregon into the settlement of Walla Walla in southeastern Washington. At one point, this trail passed close to the Devil's Sink area near Elgin, Oregon.

Mack Clifton and Johnny Arnot worked for the Tilton Freight Company based in Boise. The two drivers made regular runs from the busy supply town to Walla Walla, well over two hundred miles to the northwest. During one of the long trips, the two men spent the night camped just outside of Elgin. Following breakfast the next morning, the drivers hitched their six-horse team to the heavily laden wagon and put them on the trail toward their Washington destination. About an hour after leaving Elgin, the men spotted a log lying across the trail just ahead. Since the log blocked their passage, Clifton pulled the wagon to a halt and Arnot jumped down to try to remove the obstruction. Just as Arnot reached the log, a shot rang out from the nearby woods and the driver fell dead, a bullet through his heart.

Within a matter of a few seconds, five masked men ran from the adjacent woods and surrounded the freight wagon, ordering Clifton to keep his hands above his head and away from the shotgun lying on the wagon seat.

While the surviving driver was held at gunpoint, two of the bandits climbed into the back of the freight wagon and rummaged among the goods. After several minutes, one of them pulled a tarpaulin from a large object and, with the help of two of his companions, removed a heavy chest from the wagon and lowered it to the ground.

After breaking the lock that held the lid of the chest closed, the robbers opened it up, revealing hundreds of gold coins lying within. Clifton looked upon the huge fortune with great surprise, for he was unaware he was transporting anything other than tools and minings supplies.

After placing the coins into several saddlebags, the bandits removed the log from the trail and ordered driver Clifton to continue on his way. As the frightened man lashed his team toward Walla Walla, he turned and watched the robbers ride away into the valley of Devil's Sink.

On reaching the next settlement, a tiny cluster of shacks about twenty miles farther up the road, Clifton stopped and sent word of the robbery to law enforcement authorities in the area who took up pursuit immediately.

It was the afternoon of the day following the robbery that a posse of some twenty men, led by the sheriff from Elgin, entered the Devil's Sink region. Within minutes, they encountered the outlaw encampment and ordered the occupants to throw down their guns and surrender.

In response, the vastly outnumbered outlaws fired upon the posse members, wounding several with the first volley. For the next hour and a half, bandits and lawmen engaged in a gun battle that claimed lives on both sides: Two of the outlaws were killed; three of the posse members were killed and four wounded.

Just before sundown, the three outlaws that remained alive suddenly broke and ran to their tethered horses, mounted, and attempted to escape down the trail past the lawmen. The deputies, firing at close range from behind the protection of boulders and trees, shot each one of the outlaws from their saddles.

After examining the fallen desperadoes, it was discovered that one of them, a youth named Johnny Bailey, was still alive but bleeding badly.

The sheriff ordered a contingent of the deputies to transport the dead and wounded men, along with the prisoner, back to Elgin. The remaining lawmen undertook a search of the campsite for the stolen $60,000 in gold coins. The sheriff and his followers searched until darkness fell and set up camp for the night. As soon as they finished breakfast the next morning, they continued their search but were dismayed at finding nothing, not even a single coin.

When the sheriff finally arrived back at Elgin, he immediately sought out his prisoner so he could interrogate him as to the whereabouts of the gold shipment. Bailey was found lying on a cot in the office of the town doctor, barely clinging to life. The physician told the sheriff that the young man had lost a great deal of blood and was not expected to live much longer.

Leaning close to Bailey, the sheriff asked the wounded man what was done with the gold shipment. Bailey, though suffering terribly from at least three bullet wounds, smiled at the sheriff, rose up on his elbows, and spit in the lawman's face.

Before leaving, the sheriff placed a guard at Bailey's bedside with instructions to listen closely to the mutterings of the dying youth in the hope that some information about the location of the hidden gold would be passed.

The next morning, a nurse arrived to clean and dress the patient's wound. While she was occupied with her duties, the guard went out for breakfast.

After the guard left, Bailey pulled the nurse close to him and, in a whispering and halting voice, told her that the gold, still loaded in saddlebags, was tossed into the deepest of the two sinkholes located at Devil's Sink. He told her that if she would help him get away, he would retrieve the gold and share it with her. The nurse pretended to go along with the plan out of fear that Bailey would harm her, but as she proceeded with changing his bandages, the badly wounded outlaw suddenly died.

After alerting the doctor and the sheriff, the nurse related the dying outlaw's words.

The next day, the sheriff led a group consisting of five deputies back out to Devil's Sink. They rode to Big Sink, the larger of the two small lakes, and began probing the depths with long poles, none of which struck bottom.

One of the deputies, the only one of the group who could swim, removed his clothes and dove into the cold water of the Big Sink. About thirty seconds later, he broke the surface and proclaimed that the sink was bottomless. Believing the $60,000 in gold coins was unrecoverable, the sheriff and his men left the valley, abandoning the search.

For years, the tale of the fortune in gold coins lost in the depths of the "bottomless" lake has lured hundreds of treasure seekers into the Devil's Sink area. Some of the more adventurous searchers entered the waters of Big Sink, each announcing that, indeed, it was bottomless.

Years later, when underwater diving gear became available, several treasure hunters employed some of the equipment to search for the lost treasure in the Big Sink. It was eventually learned that, not only was the sink not bottomless, it actually wasn't very deep at all. No treasure was found, however.

In 1972, a diver named Hank Pillow, a salvage operator from Seattle, camped in the Devil's Sink region for nearly a week while he searched for the lost treasure with state-of-the-art, sophisticated self-contained underwater breathing apparatus.

Pillow claimed that the numerous floods that had ravaged the canyon since the time the gold was dropped into Big Sink more than a hundred years earlier had deposited a thick layer of silt and debris on the bottom, making recovery of the coins difficult. In addition, Pillow announced that the leather saddlebags containing the gold coins had long since rotted to shreds and pieces, spilling the valuable contents into the soft silt where the heavy metal coins quickly and easily sank to unknown depths in the soft muck.

During an interview with a Portland, Oregon, newspaper reporter, Pillow explained that, with high-resolution underwater metal-detecting equipment and an efficient dredge, the treasure could possibly be recovered. In fact, he relayed plans to return to the sinkhole in a few months to conduct a major recovery operation.

The reporter asked Pillow what proof he could offer that the treasure was still to be found in the sinkhole. In response, the diver held up a piece of a rotted leather saddlebag and three gold coins he claimed he plucked from the silt that covered the bottom of Big Sink.

Pillow never returned to the Devil's Sink region to recover the gold. Several weeks following his return to Seattle, he was killed in a freak accident while working on a salvage operation in Puget Sound.

Since then, no further attempts have been made to recover the fortune in gold coins that still lies on the murky bottom of the pit at Devil's Sink.

Sterling Creek Valley Lode

Somewhere in Sterling Creek Valley in southwestern Oregon lies a deposit of gold apparently seen and excavated by only one man. When the discoverer of this rich lode died about a year later, he took the secret of the location with him, and for the past 130 years treasure hunters have entered and searched the region trying to find it.

Jacob Roudebush arrived in Oregon from Indiana sometime during the mid-1850s and tried his hand at several occupations—sawmill operator, teamster, clerk, trapper, and prospector. During his many prospecting forays into the Klamath Mountains and Cascade Range, Roudebush became quite knowledgeable about the geology of the area and occasionally found some gold in small quantities.

Months of living in the cold, rain-drenched Oregon mountains, however, left Jacob Roudebush weakened with severe respiratory problems. On visiting a physician one day while in Grants Pass, the prospector learned he had consumption and was advised to stay out of the mountains. The doctor told him that long walks and exercise in the drier air of the lowlands might prolong his life somewhat.

Roudebush eventually settled into a small cabin not far from Sterling Creek Valley. Each morning he awoke, breakfasted, and set out on a three-mile hike up into the valley, hoping to charge his weakened lungs with the clean air. During these walks, Roudebush would often pause to observe the wildlife at play and listen to the singing of the birds. His walks brought him a certain sense of peace and relaxation, and he looked forward to them.

One morning as Roudebush paused to rest up on a fallen log, he watched a small herd of deer browsing along the edge of a small glade in the valley. Presently, he caught a glint of sunlight reflecting from a rock outcrop low on the opposite wall of the canyon. With his prospector's sense of curiosity still healthy and active, Roudebush crossed the glade and climbed the gently sloping, lightly vegetated slope to the source of the glint.

Laboriously, Roudebush climbed up to an eighteen-inch-wide, sinuous seam of quartz that snaked horizontally across the exposed granite wall, its path tracing a rift in the matrix likely created eons earlier by a great earthquake. In this bright, somewhat pinkish, layer of quartz, Roudebush identified nuggets of gold.

With his pocketknife, Roudebush dug several of the nuggets from the quartz and examined them closely, turning them over and over in his weathered fingers. Poking and slicing the small nuggets with his knife, he determined they were quite pure and most likely worth a lot of money. Examining the extensive gold-filled quartz seam, Roudebush judged a great fortune in the precious ore could easily be dug from the source in a relatively short time.

The following morning found Roudebush back at the site of the quartz seam with a miner's pick and a canvas sack. Because his anticipation was high, Roudebush hiked out to the location at a brisk pace and, as a result, was weak and breathless when he finally arrived. After resting for thirty minutes, he proceeded to chop away at the quartz vein, releasing several ounces of the gold nuggets.

Only ten minutes of work quickly exhausted the consumptive, and once again, Roudebush was forced to halt and rest. During this respite, the old prospector realized his diminishing health would be a serious handicap relative to his extraction of the gold in this rich deposit. Taking the few nuggets he was able to remove, Roudebush placed them in his sack, hoisted his pick, and returned to his cabin.

The next morning, Roudebush was again at the site, but this time he spent nearly an hour digging out the gold. This time, however, he paced himself, stopping often to catch his breath, and using only his pocketknife to gently pry out only the small nuggets close to the surface. At the end of that time, he placed the few ounces of gold he extracted into one shirt pocket and took a leisurely walk home.

Over the next few months, Roudebush would stop at the quartz seam during his morning walk, dig out a few small nuggets, and return to his cabin where he placed them in the canvas bag that he kept hidden under his bed. As time passed, he accumulated a considerable fortune in gold.

A year after Roudebush was diagnosed with consumption, his health took a turn for the worse. Various medicines recommended by the physician had little or no effect, and soon he became bedridden, unable to continue his daily walks into the Sterling Creek Valley.

One of Jake Roudebush's friends during this time was a neighbor named John Saltmarsh. Saltmarsh occasionally shared food with the prospector and looked in on him from time to time. As Roudebush's health declined, Saltmarsh often stopped by the cabin with food and other items needed by the sick man.

One afternoon, while Saltmarsh was cutting and splitting enough firewood to get Roudebush through the winter, the tired, weakened man called out to him from his bed. On entering the sick man's room, Saltmarsh could plainly see that his friend was having difficulty breathing and was struggling to talk.

Presently, Roudebush was able to instruct Saltmarsh to pull a canvas sack out from underneath the bed. As he did so, Saltmarsh was surprised at the great weight of the bag relative to its size. When Roudebush told his friend to open it, Saltmarsh was startled to find it was nearly filled to the top with gold nuggets!

Slowly, haltingly, and with great difficulty, Roudebush told Saltmarsh about the discovery of the gold-filled seam of quartz in the Sterling Creek Valley. As he did not expect to live much longer, Roudebush presented the sack of gold nuggets to his friend in gratitude for the care offered during the previous months of sickness.

Two days later, Jacob Roudebush, weakened to the point of complete helplessness, was transported to a hospital in Jacksonville where, exactly one hundred days later, he died.

Soon afterward, John Saltmarsh converted Roudebush's gold to cash and lived comfortably for a number of years. Unfortunately, numerous bad investments threatened to plunge him into a state of near-poverty. On the brink of bankruptcy, Saltmarsh decided to return to the Sterling Creek Valley and locate the seam of gold-filled pink quartz described by his late friend. Though Saltmarsh searched the valley for several weeks, he was never able to locate the rich vein.

Months passed, and word of Roudebush's gold discovery spread throughout much of southwestern Oregon. Before long, dozens of prospectors and treasure hunters were searching the Sterling Creek Valley hoping to locate the elusive ore. For several years this activity continued, but the seam was never found. One prospector, while setting up camp just off the main trail that entered the valley, discovered a small canvas sack filled with gold nuggets lying next to the trunk of a large tree. It is believed that the gold belonged to Roudebush who, finding it to heavy to transport out of the valley in his weakened condition, had simply abandoned it.

The discovery of the sack of gold renewed interest in the valley, and in no time at all more gold hunters arrived. Nothing, however, was ever found.

It may be that the searcher for the elusive gold seam in one side of the canyon wall may get lucky only if, like Roudebush, he happens to catch a glint of the morning sun shining on the thin outcrop of pink quartz while seated on a fallen log near the edge of a small glade.

Lost Saddlebags
of Gold Coins

As late as the 1890s, Union County, a region of mountains, foothills, and low-lying meadows located in northeastern Oregon, was still somewhat sparsely settled. The rich, timbered slopes of the Blue Mountains offered opportunities for lumbermen, and the lush, grassy meadows were beginning to lure cattlemen into the area, but for the most part, this somewhat remote and isolated locale boasted few settlements of any significant size.

One of the first to establish a cattle ranch in the area was William Bennett, an immigrant from New York, homesteaded near the tiny settlement of Mount Sinai. Because he was a dedicated worker bent on making a good living in this new promised land, because he was willing to spend as many as eighteen hours a day in the saddle, and because there was very little competition in the area at the time, Bennett prospered over the years, growing relatively wealthy.

Ophelia Bennett, wife of William and older by three years, was unable to bear children, a circumstance that the rancher openly regretted and lamented. Until it was discovered that Ophelia was barren, William Bennett long held dreams of raising a crop of fine sons and daughters to help him on the ranch, to contribute to its growth, and to continue to see to its progress and success long after he passed away.

In part because he was childless, Bennett took a strong liking to a young man, the son of a neighbor who operated a small ranch close to the mountain slopes. Lynn Hill was only seven years of age when he and rancher Bennett became close friends, and the young man would occasionally ride out to the large ranch to help with roundup and branding and spend time listening to stories at the knee of the homesteader.

The years passed. World War I broke out, and the nation's military called for the services of Lynn Hill, now twenty years old. Before leaving for basic training, Hill visited the Bennett ranch to say goodbye to William and Ophelia. As Hill and the rancher were chatting in the spacious family room of the large, fine rock-and-log home, Bennett, now an old man, motioned the younger one over to a set of bookcases against one wall. After pulling a section of the bookcases aside, Bennett removed two heavy saddlebags from the rounded niche built into the exposed rock wall. After dragging the saddlebags across the floor and over to the middle of the room, Bennett opened them and showed Hill what the young man later described as an "incredible fortune in gold coins." Bennett explained to Hill that there were several more bags just like these two, all filled with gold coins and buried in a secret location just beyond the house. As Hill gaped in stunned amazement at the hundreds of coins in the saddlebags, Bennett continued to speak.

The rancher told young Hill that these coins, as well as others he had buried, represented much of his accrued wealth, his income from the highly successful operation of the large cattle ranch. Should he die, he said, the sale of the ranch would ensure his wife's financial security. Because Hill was such a fine, hard-working young man with strong principles, he explained, he wanted to share his wealth with him. His head swimming with the disbelief of so great a fortune, Hill tried hard to focus his attention as Bennett described where he had buried the other saddlebags filled with gold coins.

Tomorrow, he told Hill, he would tote these very bags lying before them on the floor to a secret location where he cached his fortune. To find it, he continued, one had to go a couple of hundred yards due north of the big ranch house where a large, flat stone about the size of a wagon wheel would be found. Exactly thirty-five feet northeast of this rock, next to a low bush, was where three other bags of gold were buried. Bennett told Hill that if he was dead by the time the young man returned from the war, the gold was his, a gift for his important friendship.

In 1918, Lynn Hill was released from military service, and he promptly returned to Union County. On arriving, he was greeted with the news that his old friend, rancher Bennett, had passed away the previous year.

Allowing several weeks to pass while settling in at his home, Lynn Hill finally traveled to the Bennett homestead. Months earlier, Ophelia Bennett had moved away to live with relatives in San Francisco. Before leaving, she had the big house boarded up. Starting at the north side of the ranch house, Hill paced off two hundred yards and stopped to search for the large, flat stone Bennett said would be found there. It was not there! Hill returned to the house and paced the distance once again, stopping at approximately the same location. After marking his position, Hill walked about, searching for the stone, but was unable to find it. As he surveyed the immediate area looking for the low-growing bush identified by Bennett, he found not one, but dozens of bushes that likely had grown up in the untended pasture during the past few years. Discouraged, he returned home.

On at least a dozen occasions, Lynn Hill returned to the Bennett homestead to search for the trove of gold coins, but each time he came away with nothing, unable to locate the old rancher's secret hiding place.

Years later, Hill learned from one of Bennett's former ranch hands that the large flat stone north of the house was moved, as a result of instructions from Ophelia, to a location near the barn where it was used to cover an old well.

With the passage of decades, the old Bennett ranch house has long since rotted away and tumbled down. The Union County region of northeastern Oregon has seen great growth in population and tourism.

Searching through the old records in the Union County courthouse, it is possible to determine the exact location of William Bennett's old homestead. Once in the area, it would be an easy task to determine the site of the old ranch house, as the large rocks that made up the foundation and walls will still be apparent. From there, pacing off two hundred yards to the north, followed by another thirty-five feet to the northeast would place one close to the old rancher's buried treasure. With an adequate metal detector, one might just find William Bennett's great fortune in buried gold coins.

The Nez Perce Gold

There exist throughout northeastern Oregon and western Idaho many tales of large gold deposits supposedly known only to Nez Perce Indians. From time to time throughout this region, members of the tribe would arrive at the various settlements to purchase food, tools, guns, and ammunition, always making payment with pieces of gold crudely mined from a stone matrix.

Merchants tried many times to learn the secret location of the Nez Perce gold, but the Indians remained silent to the question. Indians were often followed when they left town but were always successful in eluding their trackers. It was whispered about the camps and settlements that any member of the tribe who revealed the location of the gold to white men would meet with a horrible death.

The source of the Nez Perce gold remains as much a mystery today as it did more than one hundred years ago.

One of the best documented tales of Nez Perce gold involves an Indian named John Cash-Cash. It has been told that Cash-Cash was once a noted warrior during the so-called Nez Perce War with the white settlers. When the tribe was eventually subdued, Cash-Cash purchased a large tract of land near Wallowa Lake on the eastern side of the Wallowa Mountains not far from the town of Enterprise. Here, Cash-Cash settled into a quiet and peaceful family life and raised cattle.

When he had the opportunity, Cash-Cash increased the size of his ranch by adding parcels of land when they became available. Each time the Indian acquired land, he paid for it in gold, offering nuggets of great purity. Many began to notice that just before purchasing new acreage, Cash-Cash would disappear into the Wallowa Mountains for several days, always returning with several thousand dollars worth of ore.

White men who coveted Cash-Cash's source of gold sometimes watched the Indian for days, even weeks, at a time, waiting for him to make a journey into the mountains. When he did, they trailed along at a distance, hoping to discover the location of the secret mine that yielded his gold. As did the Indians who dug out the gold before him, Cash-Cash was aware that many tried to follow him, but he always covered his trail. Cash-Cash always entered the Wallowa Mountains by riding up the trail that paralleled the Lostine River, and it was generally somewhere along the middle stretch of that stream that the trackers lost him.

One of the few white men Cash-Cash associated with was a Frenchman, a trapper several years older named Henri Sebastian. Sebastian often spent several days at a time at the Cash-Cash ranch, helping his Nez Perce friend with roundup and branding. After a full day of work, the two would sit around the hearth together in the evening smoking and drinking brandy and reliving the days of their youth in the wild and untamed mountains before the arrival of so many settlers.

Years passed, and a lifetime of hard work had finally taken its toll on John Cash-Cash. Enfeebled with age and infirmity, as well as recurring pain from wounds he received as a warrior years earlier, he was no longer able to perform tasks on his ranch, except to occasionally ride with his herd. The old Indian now spent most of his days in bed. Sebastian, now in his eighties, also found it difficult to get around but would ride out to his friend's ranch once a week to visit.

One evening as Cash-Cash and Sebastian shared a meal, the Indian and his friend talked about the Nez Perce gold.

Cash-Cash acknowledged he would not live much longer and would have no more use for wealth. He told Sebastian that because he was such a good and loyal friend, he would reveal the location of the mine to him, a site long held secret by the tribe. Following supper, Cash-Cash drew a map to the gold mine on the inside front cover of an old, tattered book. As he sketched in trails and landmarks, he provided directions to Sebastian. The gold, he said, was taken from an exposed quartz seam deep in the Wallowa Mountains, a place where no white man had ever entered.

When Cash-Cash finished with the map, he handed the book to Sebastian, and gave him a warning. "If my people catch you anywhere near the gold, they will torture and kill you. Then they will find me and kill me. Be careful, my friend."

Sebastian promised Cash-Cash he would not make any attempt to find the gold as long as his friend lived. With that, the two said goodnight and Sebastian rode back to his cabin. It was the last time he saw John Cash-Cash alive, for two days later the old Indian suffered a heart attack while riding among his herd of cattle. He was dead when neighbors found him.

Several weeks later, Sebastian, leading a packhorse piled high with supplies, rode up the Lostine River and into the Wallowa Mountains. Townspeople who saw him ride away claimed he was carrying a book and intently referring to some writing on the inside front cover.

Nearly a month passed before Sebastian returned to the town of Enterprise. He walked into the mercantile and, smiling, dumped a leather poke filled with gold nuggets onto the counter and purchased some mining tools, beans, sugar, coffee, and expensive cigars.

As the shopkeeper measured out the gold on a scale, customers, both white and Indian, crowded around to stare at the old man's ore. When some of the white men asked Sebastian how he came by this gold, the Frenchman told them he had finally discovered the location of the secret

Nez Perce gold. He also told them he was returning to the mountains to fill another two or three pokes of the almost pure ore. Sebastian refused several offers of help from the men.

Meanwhile, in a far corner of the store, three Nez Perce Indians listened quietly and intently to the conversation between the white men and the old trapper. Later, when Sebastian carried his new purchases out of the mercantile, loaded them onto his horse, and rode away, the Indians, without a word, paid for their few purchases and left.

Two days later, Sebastian was once again seen leaving for the Wallowa Mountains, riding alone and leading a horse packed with his newly purchased supplies. Several Wallowa citizens waved at the old trapper as he rode by. He told them he would return in a month.

When a month had elapsed, Wallowa residents began to inquire about the old trapper. Another week passed, and a search party was organized. They rode up the Lostine River canyon in search of the old man but found no sign of him. A few days later, it was reported in town that a Nez Perce Indian was seen with Henri Sebastian's horse and saddle. When several residents went to investigate, they could not find the Indian.

Though the truth may never be known, it was long rumored around northeastern Oregon that the Nez Perce caught Henri Sebastian at the secret location of their gold and killed him. When some tribal members were questioned, they only responded by telling the inquisitors that their gold was always watched.

Even today, it is whispered among residents of Wallowa, Enterprise, La Grande, Pendleton, and other northeastern Oregon towns that the Nez Perce gold does indeed exist, that it lies somewhere deep in the Wallowa Mountains, and that it continues to be guarded by the Indians. During the 1970s, two different treasure hunting expeditions entered the Wallowas in search of the gold. One party returned and reported having no success whatsoever, even publicly announcing their doubts that the secret gold mine ever existed. The other party, consisting of four seasoned treasure hunters from California, disappeared completely. Search parties scoured the Wallowa Mountains for two full weeks, but all efforts to find the men proved fruitless. Their disappearance remains a deep mystery today, and some claim only the Nez Perce Indians know what happened to them.

Did the Californians discover the gold and become the most recent victims of those responsible for guarding and protecting the secret location? Many believe they were.

The Lost Ramsey
Party Gold

Peyton Ramsey learned his prospecting and mining as a young man in the California goldfields. Arriving in the Golden State in 1850 and following the thousands that migrated westward in the hope of finding their fortune in the streams and rock outcrops of California, Ramsey, only twenty years of age, joined up with a group of miners dedicated to striking it rich. Though young and inexperienced, the miners were impressed by Ramsey's desire to learn and his willingness to work hard and cooperate.

An eager and enthusiastic student, Ramsey watched and listened to his comrades, gleaning every bit of information he could on how and where to find gold. Though the party met with some successes, the competition for prospecting and mining in the California mountains was intense, and most of the potentially rich areas were already claimed.

After two years in the wilderness, Ramsey, by dint of native intelligence and highly disciplined work habits, eventually became the acknowledged leader of the group of miners. Not long after spending three months of hard work prospecting and panning for gold in the Sierra Nevadas and having nothing to show for it, Ramsey, in his first important decision as leader, suggested they abandon California and investigate the less-well-known prospects in

Oregon. Everyone agreed with him, and after packing their belongings, the group of seven miners headed out of the Sierra Nevadas and followed the trails to the Coast Range in southwestern Oregon. After several weeks of traveling, scouting, exploring, and prospecting streams and outcrops in a remote region located between the Illinois and Silver Rivers, Ramsey decided the group should concentrate on a promising quartz vein they found in a secluded canyon in the western shadow of Onion Mountain. After three weeks of digging into the quartz, one of the miners discovered a large section of it laced with rich gold. Impressed with the quantity and quality of the ore, Ramsey promised his friends they would make their fortune there and retire to a life of wealth and luxury in San Francisco before the year was out. Inspired by dreams of riches, the party threw itself into the work and in a short time had accumulated an impressive amount of gold ore.

Only one thing stood between the miners and realizing their grand dreams of wealth: the area they selected for their mining operations was populated by Indians who, at the time, were hostile to and resentful of the intrusion of white men in the region.

On the afternoon of the second day of digging out the gold, dozens of Indians armed with bows and lances began appearing on the ridge tops. Eerily silent, not moving for hours at a time, they observed the activities of the miners. Though nervous, the men continued about their work and tried to ignore the enemy presence. Each one of the miners, however, kept a loaded pistol or rifle close by just in case it was needed.

Two weeks passed, and the Ramsey party was beginning to run low on provisions. One morning, two men were sent into the forest to hunt game while two others were designated to travel to Grants Pass, the nearest settlement some thirty miles away, to purchase flour, beans, coffee, and sugar.

Late that same afternoon, one of the miners sent on the hunting expedition rode into camp. He was slumped over his saddle and bleeding profusely from an arrow wound in his chest. After he was made as comfortable as possible next to the campfire, the arrow was removed and the man haltingly and with great difficulty described how he and his companion were attacked by Indians as they tracked an elk herd up a rocky canyon about two miles northwest of the camp. The other miner was killed, and as the survivor was escaping, he was struck by the arrow. As he rode out of the canyon, he saw the Indians standing over the body of his friend.

More cautious than ever, the remaining miners went about their daily work more nervous than ever about the threat of potential Indian attack. For days, no more Indians were seen on the ridge tops, and the wounded man soon recovered. When the miners began to believe their luck was changing for the better, they gradually relaxed their guard.

Late one evening in camp, a saddled, riderless horse was spotted grazing in the narrow meadow along a nearby creek about one hundred yards away. It was immediately recognized as belonging to one of the men who was sent to Grants Pass to procure supplies. The next morning, the four remaining miners rode down the canyon to try to find the missing rider. After searching the area near the mouth of the canyon for an about an hour, one of the men discovered the bodies of their two friends. Dozens of arrows protruded from the bloated corpses of the dead miners.

Desperately low on food and fearful of continued attack from the Indians, Ramsey decided it would be prudent to load what gold they had accumulated and abandon the area for the time being, perhaps returning in the future when the threat of hostile Indians had ebbed. On returning to camp, however, they encountered even more trouble.

As the miners rounded a bend in the trail, they could see their camp in the distance. About fifteen Indians were ransacking their belongings, ripping down tents, and spilling foodstuffs onto the ground. Grabbing their fire-arms, the riders charged into camp, shooting and yelling as they drove the raiders away, killing two of them.

Quickly, the men began to gather up what belongings had not been destroyed, determined to leave this danger-ous area as soon as possible. The gold which had been mined from the quartz vein was packed into leather pan-niers and quickly tied to wooden packsaddles lashed onto three mules. Ramsey estimated the men would divide about $80,000 worth of gold when they returned to civili-zation. Keeping a wary eye out for ambush, the miners rode slowly down and out of the canyon toward Grants Pass.

After leaving the canyon, the trail led the miners across an extensive rock outcrop, a part of a low ridge that separated the drainage basins of two rivers. The smooth granite was broken only by an occasional vertical crevice, undoubtedly caused by earthquakes of long ago. Most of the cracks were only about five feet deep, but some of them extended more than twenty feet into the rock.

For two hours, not a single Indian was seen nor any unusual sounds heard, and the miners grew more relaxed. Some even holstered their pistols and daydreamed about exchanging their gold for cash when they reached town.

Suddenly, rising up out of several of the shallow rifts in the outcrop, about forty Indians unleashed a barrage of arrows and lances at the unsuspecting riders. As horses and men panicked, a circle of Indians closed in. Some of the warriors grabbed and held onto the reins of the horses and mules while others pulled the surprised and frightened men from the saddles.

Within minutes, all of the miners were killed. While several Indians removed clothing and scalps from the dead men, others took items from the saddlebags lashed to the horses and mules. Finally, the packsaddles were cut from the mules and they, along with the attached panniers filled with gold ore, were thrown into a nearby deep crevice. The bodies of the miners were then tossed into the rift atop the pile and the Indians, wearing clothing from the dead miners and leading the horses and mules, departed.

Many years passed, and leaves, pine needles, and other forest debris were blown across the exposed rock outcrop, some of it falling into the crevices. In one large and deep opening, the forest debris partially covered the skeletons of four men and the packs of gold.

In 1902, two trappers entered the Klamath Mountains and spent several weeks running lines along the Illinois and Silver Rivers. While moving from the drainage basin of one river to the other, the two men were forced to cross a low ridge and traverse a long section of bare rock outcrop. Carefully, they guided their horses and pack animals along the somewhat dangerous route, which contained many deep crevices in the exposed granite. At one point during the crossing, one of the trappers, a man named Pete Hutchins, spotted some bones at the bottom of one of the crevices. Dismounting, he lay on the edge of the crack and peered into the interior. At the bottom of the rift, he claimed, he saw the skeletal remains of at least four men. Hutchins considered climbing down into the crevice to see if he could find any identification on the bodies, but the sheer, smooth sides of the rift afforded no safe descent. The two trappers finally rode away, completely unaware of the existence of a fortune in gold ore that lay beneath the rotting bones of Peyton Ramsey and his three companions, gold that is still there, having lain undisturbed for over one hundred years.

Lost Blue Bucket Gold

One of the most mysterious and confusing tales of lost gold in the American West is the one called the Lost Blue Bucket Gold. The confusion and mystery has little to do with the existence of the gold—the ore has been seen by dozens of people. The problem lies with determining the location of this long-lost and elusive deposit of rich ore. Some researchers place the source of the gold in Nevada, others in Idaho, and a few in Utah. Contemporary investigators of the case of the Lost Blue Bucket Gold are convinced it was originally found in southeastern Oregon.

According to the story, a fantastic fortune in placer gold was accidentally discovered by a group of Oregon-bound immigrants while traveling through a small canyon near the Nevada–Oregon border. Several nuggets were collected, but no one recognized them for what they were at the time. When it was discovered later that the nuggets were gold, several immigrants returned to the area in an attempt to relocate the canyon but were unsuccessful. Today, the site of the Lost Blue Bucket Gold remains one of the greatest mysteries in America.

In 1845 a large wagon train slowly made its way along the Humboldt Trail across the extremely rugged and unpopulated terrain of northern Nevada. The train was composed of more than a hundred heavily laden wagons pulled by oxen. Most of the members of the train were bound for the rich farming country of southern Oregon, while others would travel to California. Those continuing on to Oregon parted company with the California-bound immigrants near the present-day town of Imlay and proceeded along the Applegate–Lassen trail that took them through what is now Humboldt County, Nevada, and on into Oregon.

The Applegate–Lassen Trail was more difficult than anything the immigrants had experienced thus far—much of it had been washed away as a result of recent torrential rains and they lost a great deal of time searching for routes around and across the deep gullies caused by rapid runoff. In some places, the wagons and stock had to be lowered down steep inclines using ropes and the efforts of dozens of men.

During this part of the trip, the immigrants had to be constantly on the lookout for hostile Indians for this was Paiute country. All along the trail could be found the graves of less fortunate travelers who encountered the warring Paiutes who resented the intrusion of whites into their homelands.

One morning, following a particularly difficult traverse of a steep section of trail, the wagon train proceeded through a shallow canyon located on the Nevada–Oregon border. The immigrants knew they were only a few days away from their destination, and their spirits were high. Anticipating the end of their long and arduous journey, they sang as they guided the wagons along the rocky bottom of the canyon.

As the wagons rolled along, jouncing over rocks and clattering on the bare granite floor of the canyon, the many youngsters in the party ran alongside playing in the narrow stream that paralleled the trail. Now and again the bright gleam of small shiny stones would catch the eyes of the children and they would pick them up. One child challenged another that she could find more of the shiny rocks than any of the others, and a playful contest soon evolved.

As the children excitedly gathered the gleaming yellow stones, they threw them into the wooden utility buckets that were tied to the sides of many of the wagons. The buckets, purchased in St. Louis from a manufacturer, were all painted blue and were used to haul water and various items.

The men, their attention directed toward keeping the wagons on the trail and remaining constantly on the lookout for Indians, ignored the playful antics of the children and paid no attention to the growing collections of small yellowish stones in the bottoms of several of the empty blue buckets.

Several days later, when the wagon train arrived at its destination in southern Oregon, the business of unpacking and setting up temporary shelters and housekeeping got underway. As the blue buckets were needed to carry items and transport water, those carrying the shiny stones were dumped and put into use. Some of the children managed to gather up their shiny stones before they were discarded, however, and kept them among their few personal belongings.

Several months later a party of miners stopped at the new immigrant settlement. They had recently come from a successful gold mining venture in the mountains of northern California and were on their way back east to set themselves up in business with their newfound wealth. While visiting with some of the immigrants around a campfire one evening, one of the miners observed a child playing with several small glistening stones. The light of the campfire reflected off of the yellow rocks and caught the attention of the visitor. After asking the child if he could see one of them, the miner examined the nugget closely. Presently he asked where it had come from, and the father of the child explained that the children had picked them up from the bottom of a small canyon many miles to the southeast, near the Nevada border.

The miner, holding the nugget out to the man, informed him it was the purest gold he had ever seen!

The remaining nuggets were inspected and they, like the first, were found to be gold. Other children who had also collected nuggets were asked to bring them forward, and in each case they likewise proved to be gold.

Several of the settlers, excited about the prospect of a great fortune in gold awaiting them on the floor of that shallow canyon several days' ride to the southeast, immediately began preparations to return. Within the next two days, a party of several men had outfitted themselves and rode out of the settlement to try to relocate the gold-filled canyon.

The expedition was doomed from the start. One evening while camping in a thicket along a small stream in southeastern Oregon, most of their horses were stolen by Indians. Undeterred, however, they proceeded with several of them on foot.

As they approached the area where they believed they would find the canyon, the men were set upon by Indians and barely escaped with their lives. Completely frightened, they returned to the settlement and vowed never to return to the canyon again.

While the enthusiasm of the settlers for locating the gold had dimmed somewhat, their penchant for relating the story did not, and many a visitor to the immigrant settlement heard the tale of the Lost Blue Bucket Gold. Several visitors who heard the story made attempts to find the canyon but were turned back by hostile Indians, scarcity of water, and sometimes just plain bad luck.

One day, several years later, a physician visited the immigrant settlement and remained for a few days. As with most visitors, he was told the tale of the Lost Blue Bucket Gold. When they had finished with their story, however, the townsfolk were treated to an even more fascinating one by the doctor.

The physician had recently spent several months in Paiute country in northeastern Nevada near the Black Rock and Granite Ranges treating soldiers, settlers, and even Indians for various wounds and ailments. The physician had a large gold nugget attached to his watch fob and one day, while treating a Paiute Indian for an infection, pulled out the timepiece to check the hour. On seeing the gold nugget, the Indian expressed interest. When the doctor explained what it was, the Indian told the doctor of a canyon located several days' ride to the north where nuggets such as this could be found in abundance in the little stream that trickled through the cut. The description of the canyon provided by the Indian matched those given by the settlers and is believed to be near the Oregon–Nevada border.

Paiutes occasionally visited old Fort Bidwell in northeastern California to obtain supplies. In many cases the Indians paid for their purchases with gold nuggets. When asked where they obtained the gold, the Indians always pointed eastward and told of a canyon where the nuggets could be easily picked up out of the shallow stream that flowed along the bottom. Several traders at the fort attempted to follow the Indians where they departed, but the Paiutes proved too elusive.

The Lost Blue Bucket Gold has been the object of hundreds of expeditions and search parties into southeastern Oregon for well over a hundred years. Some come out of the region with a bit of gold, but history has yet to record if the gold-rich canyon through which the immigrants passed in 1845 has ever been relocated.

With the passage of time, much of the original route of the Applegate–Lassen trail has been lost. Should the old trail be rediscovered using documents and journals, many suggest it would not help much in relocating the canyon for, in the intervening years, the region in question has been subjected to violent flash flooding and earthquakes, which have rearranged much of the landscape and topography from what it was 150 years ago.

That there is gold in the region has been substantiated many times. Prospectors and miners have located the precious ore in various places throughout much of southern Oregon and northern Nevada, but the canyon containing the Lost Blue Bucket Gold has always eluded the searchers.

The search, as well as the mystery, continues.

Ed Schieffelin's Lost Lode

One of the most famous prospector-miners in the history of North America was Ed Schieffelin. Normally associated with the extremely rich and highly publicized silver discoveries in Arizona and the founding of the town of Tombstone, Schieffelin eventually retired a wealthy man to Oregon, where he discovered one of the richest deposits of gold ever found. Before he was able to organize a serious attempt at extracting the gold from this site, Schieffelin died, leaving the location of the rich lode one of Oregon's greatest mysteries.

Those who have studied the life of this truly remarkable entrepreneur all agree that Ed Schieffelin was destined to become a miner. At the age of twelve, the youngster ran away from his Jackson County, Oregon, home to join a party of veteran prospectors and miners who traveled into Idaho's Salmon River valley to pan for gold. As the years passed, Schieffelin roamed throughout much of the Rocky Mountain West, always searching, always prospecting for the rich deposit of gold or silver he always believed he would eventually find. Wherever Schieffelin went, he studied the prospecting and mining techniques of those around him, ever alert to newer and better ways to locate and excavate ore. He listened intently to the advice offered by veteran geologists and miners, and by the time Schieffelin was twenty-one years old, he was regarded by many as an expert on minerals and their extraction.

Schieffelin experienced some successes, but for many years his discoveries amounted to just barely enough to keep him in food and supplies and undertaking his next mining venture. Sometimes he found nothing and went hungry. Once, he was so broke he hired on as a scout for the United States Army in Fort Huachuca, Arizona. While out on a scouting mission one day, Schieffelin spotted an outcrop bearing an extremely high silver content. He dug out some samples, had them assayed, and discovered they were quite rich. When he informed a fellow scout that he intended to quit the army and mine silver in Apache country, his friend told him all he would ever find there would be his tombstone. After weeks of hard work, Schieffelin eventually located the mother lode of the silver deposits in the region. He immediately undertook a complex yet thorough mining operation, and during the next few years succeeded in removing $75,000,000 worth of silver ore before he quit. As the riches were dug from the rock, a town sprang up around Schieffelin's discovery, a town he eventually named Tombstone.

Schieffelin's silver discovery made him a multimillionaire. While the successful miner reveled working at his enterprises, he cared little for the wild and lawless town of Tombstone. Eventually, tiring of the growing violence, he sold out his interest in the mines and decided to travel to parts of the nation he had not yet seen. He visited Washington, D.C., New York, Pittsburgh, and Chicago. He dined in fine restaurants, drank expensive wines, and attended fancy balls and concerts. While he enjoyed many aspects of the cultured life, Schieffelin soon realized urban living generally did not appeal to him. Longing to return to prospecting and mining, he traveled to Alaska to investigate the possibilities of finding gold in that relatively undeveloped yet promising land.

Schieffelin's Alaska venture yielded few successes and he soon lost interest and moved to San Francisco where he married and tried to settle once again into city life.

It didn't take long for Schieffelin to remember all of the reasons he disliked living in town. He missed the excitement of prospecting for ore. Soon he moved his family into the tiny settlement of Cornelius, Oregon, where he bought a ranch and went into business raising cattle with his two brothers, Eff and Jay.

Long fascinated with what he thought was great potential for finding gold in the southern Cascade Range, Schieffelin often traveled into southwestern Oregon where he spent weeks alone exploring the canyons, ridges, and outcrops near the South Umpqua River. Encouraged by some promising outcrops he found, the miner eventually built a small cabin near Moore Creek, a tributary to the South Umpqua. His nearest neighbor was a farmer named Jackson who lived about five miles away on Days Creek. Jackson also served as postmaster for the region, and about once a week Schieffelin would walk the five miles to his neighbor's cabin to pick up his mail. The two men became good friends and looked forward to the weekly visits. Occasionally, Jackson would hike or ride a mule up to Schieffelin's place and the two men would spend hours sitting in front of the rock hearth talking about mining, hunting, and politics. During one conversation, Schieffelin told Jackson he was searching throughout this part of the range for gold and that he had a good feeling that plenty of it could be found.

Schieffelin would journey to the South Umpqua River and live in his cabin for several weeks at a time while he prospected the region. One day, he walked to an area on a nearby ridge that separated the drainage basins of Days Creek and Coffee Creek. As he was reclining against the bole of a large tree smoking his pipe, Schieffelin noticed an exposed formation of rust-colored quartz nearby, a thick vein that had intruded through the granite of the ridge. Growing interested in the curious-looking quartz, he hiked back to the cabin, selected some tools, and returned to the seam on the ridge. After digging into the vein to a depth

71

of about eighteen inches, Schieffelin was surprised to discover that its rust color gave over to a blue-tinted quartz. To his utter amazement, this blue quartz was densely speckled with tiny bits of gold.

During the second week of May 1897, it occurred to Jackson that Schieffelin had not shown up to retrieve his mail for about ten days. Concerned his friend might be sick or injured, the postmaster placed his wife in charge and struck out for Schieffelin's cabin.

After crossing a low ridge and looking down into the little valley where Schieffelin's cabin was located, Jackson noticed was that there wasn't any smoke curling out of the chimney. Assuming his friend wasn't home, Jackson approached the cabin with the intent of leaving a note. As he did, he spotted Schieffelin's body lying across the front stoop.

From a quick examination of the corpse, Jackson deduced Schieffelin had been dead for several days. Because there were no visible wounds and no sign of a struggle, he presumed the old miner had passed away as a result of natural causes.

Jackson walked around to the back of the cabin and found Schieffelin's crucible—a small, shallow porcelain trough used for melting and calcining ore samples. Poking through the debris lying in the bottom of the crucible, Jackson found some dust and rock his friend had apparently crushed shortly before he died. His curiosity was aroused by the glint of yellow metal in the dust. Jackson carried a bucketful of water from the nearby creek and poured it gently into the crucible. After washing away most of the rock crystals and silt, he stared at several pieces of the shiny metal that remained. It was gold!

Before returning to Days Creek, Jackson entered the small cabin and looked around. Almost immediately, he found Schieffelin's diary. The last entry in the leather-bound book read: *Found it at last! Richer than Tombstone ever hoped to be.*

Jackson sent word to the sheriff at Canyonville, and soon he, along with the county coroner and justice of the peace, arrived at Schieffelin's cabin, where they concluded the miner had died from a heart attack.

Days later, Schieffelin's brother, Eff, arrived at Days Creek and listened as Jackson related the discovery of the body and the findings of the coroner. Jackson handed Schieffelin's gold samples over to Eff, who had them assayed. When the report returned a few weeks later, all were amazed to discover the gold was valued at $2,000 per ton, an incredibly high value for that time. Eff summoned his brother Jay, and together the two men searched the ridges and valleys near Ed's cabin for the source of the rich gold ore. Throughout the area, they found abandoned campsites, probably used by Ed Schieffelin, but no gold was ever located.

Jackson was convinced that Ed Schieffelin found the gold-filled blue quartz not far from the old miner's cabin. After Eff and Jay gave up and returned to their respective homes, the postmaster spent many hours riding his mule across the ridges and up and down the canyons near Schieffelin's old place in search of the gold.

One afternoon, Jackson found a curious-looking vein of rust-colored quartz on a low ridge less than two miles from Schieffelin's cabin. He dug around in the vein for several minutes, but not finding any color, he eventually abandoned it and searched elsewhere.

Had Jackson dug a few inches deeper into the vein, he likely would have encountered the blue-tinted quartz containing the rich gold found by Schieffelin.

In the years since the founder of Tombstone died, many have searched the region around Days Creek, Coffee Creek, and South Umpqua River, but none have located the source of Ed Schieffelin's gold.

The Curious Sir Francis Drake Treasure

One of the most curious lost treasures ever associated with the state of Oregon involves a cache of gold and silver ornaments and artifacts—five large chests in all—allegedly buried by the noted explorer Sir Francis Drake. This horde, believed to be worth several million dollars, is surrounded by mystery. Drake, after transporting the treasure hundreds of miles from South America to the Oregon coast, suddenly decided to bury it in a remote location. His motivations for doing so have never been learned, and it is not known whether or not he ever intended to return for it. If that was his desire, it was never fulfilled. Though some of the treasure has been found, it is believed that most of it is still hidden near a popular coastal town in southwestern Oregon.

Sir Francis Drake was one of England's most well-known mariners, a seafaring adventurer and explorer who carved out a significant place in history. Though he was placed in charge of hundreds of British mariners, some scholars considered Drake little more than a ruthless pirate, bent on increasing the size of his personal wealth and enhancing his fame. Nevertheless, Drake was a skilled navigator, fighter, and leader of men, and achieved overseas expansion by running roughshod over the Spanish navy and freeing the Atlantic of its dominance.

Drake was only the second man to circumnavigate the world, a feat which he accomplished between 1577 and 1580. During the Pacific leg of his famous voyage, he was sailing his vessel, the Golden Hind, northward along the Peruvian coast when he encountered a Spanish ship. Challenged by the Spaniards, Drake's forces engaged the aggressor and, following a brief battle, captured the Spanish vessel, which turned out to be filled with treasure sacked from numerous Incan villages. After loading the treasure into the Golden Hind, Drake continued northward to California, which he claimed for Queen Elizabeth I and named New Albion. Eventually, Drake navigated the treasure-filled ship into the harbor in San Francisco Bay, where he intended to remain for several days while his boat was overhauled and his men rested.

During the two weeks the Golden Hind was tied up at the dock, Drake and his companions enjoyed the taverns and other diversions of this wild and rowdy port while laborers loaded the ship with goods and supplies. While trunks filled with provisions and barrels filled with fresh water were carried up the gangplank and stored in the hold, two dozen men armed with knives and cutlasses stood guard over the fabulous Incan treasure.

When Drake returned to the ship, he supervised loading of the treasure into several large trunks—at least five. These stout, wooden seagoing cases, reinforced with copper corners and bound tightly with thick leather straps, carried a king's ransom in artifacts, idols, and jewelry fashioned from gold and silver and studded with emeralds and other precious stones. Into some of the chests, Drake also placed gold Spanish coins, part of the booty taken from the enemy ship.

Early one morning around sunrise several days following the loading of the supplies, the Golden Hind quietly sailed out of San Francisco Bay on a northward course that paralleled the coast.

For reasons that have never been clear, Drake anchored the *Golden Hind* in shallow water just off the Oregon coast near the present-day town of Gold Beach. Very carefully, each of the heavy treasure-filled trunks was loaded into a rowboat and transported to shore. Several stout sailors carried the chests from the rowboats to a grassy sward that extended from the level of high tide to a rock outcrop several hundred yards to the east. Near the middle of this sward and separated by several yards, the men dug five deep and wide excavations. When Drake was satisfied with the placement and depth of the holes, he ordered a treasure chest lowered into each one. The holes were then filled in. When the job of caching the treasure was complete, the sailors returned to the vessel, raised the anchor, and in a matter of only a few hours, the *Golden Hind* was once again underway. The fact that the treasure was so carefully hidden in this deserted area strongly suggests that Drake fully intended to return for it, but he never did, and for more than 360 years the treasure lay undisturbed.

In the 1940s, a farmer who owned a plot of fertile land located between Highway 101 and the shore near the present-day town of Gold Beach, Oregon, was plowing his field and preparing it for planting. Each year, the farmer eked out a meager living for himself and his family with his few acres of garden crops.

On this cool morning, as the farmer chucked at the mules that pulled the plow, he guided the metal point along a straight line, cutting a furrow through the giving earth. Suddenly, he snapped to a stop when the tool snagged on an unseen object, something lying just below the surface. Investigating, the farmer dug into the soft earth and found several rotted pieces from what appeared to have been a large wooden trunk, buried many years earlier. As he removed the broken and weathered pieces of the chest, he found the remains of copper fittings, small nails, and portions of leather straps. As he excavated more of the dirt, the farmer was startled to find several ornaments and small statues fashioned from gold and silver! In addition, pieces of jewelry, as well as Spanish coins, were scattered among the artifacts.

Following this incredible discovery, the farmer called in several professional archeologists to examine and evaluate the artifacts and coins, all of which were clearly very old. The coins were quickly identified as being of Spanish origin, but confusion initially reigned regarding the gold and silver objects, for the pieces could not be identified by any of the so-called experts. Most agreed, however, that the majority of them had religious significance. During the next eighteen months, while the contents of the unearthed trunk were being studied, two more similar chests, each filled with great treasures, were found in the same area.

Eventually, the famous archeologist, Emil Plotkin, was invited from New York to examine the unidentified treasures. Plotkin, who served as advisor and consultant to several important museums, had spent years studying Peruvian ruins and artifacts. Shortly after arriving at Gold Beach, he immediately recognized the unearthed pieces as being of Incan origin, even identifying the specific gods to which each of them paid tribute.

Opinions varied as to how the trunkloads of Peruvian treasure came to be buried along a portion of the south-western Oregon shore, but conclusions were difficult to come by. While experts and amateurs alike mulled over possible scenarios relative to the origin and circumstances involving this fantastic treasure, several local Indians came forward with their own version of the origin of the amazing cache.

According to Indian legend, a large and strange boat had once appeared offshore near what is now Gold Beach. From this vessel disembarked strange men wearing strange clothing. After removing small boats from the large one and rowing them to shore, the strangers interred five heavy containers and departed.

Other scholars, familiar with the travels and exploits of Sir Francis Drake, filled in some of the missing elements and the story began to crystallize. Though the mystery of the origin of the treasure has been solved, another—and perhaps even greater—mystery relates to the location of the two trunks that have not yet been unearthed. It is presumed by researchers that they were buried in locations not far from where the others were found. With the passage of time and the unfortunate loss of written records relating to the three chests that were discovered, no one today is entirely certain of the location of the discoveries.

The two remaining chests are still there, lying just a few inches below the surface where they were buried more than four hundred years ago. Once a flat, grass-covered area, the region was farmed for many years. Today it is possible that urban development may have encroached upon the site, perhaps even covered it. Many treasure hunters are discouraged by such things and are reluctant to undertake a search in an area that may be cloaked in concrete or asphalt. But the likelihood that several million dollars' worth of gold and silver Incan artifacts are still interred only inches below the surface is great, and many consider such a prize to be worth the effort.

Buried Pirate Treasure on Oregon Shore

Many years ago—no one knows exactly when—a sailing vessel, suffering from a severe leak in the hull, entered a small bay on the Oregon coast near present-day Three Rocks Beach in the northern part of Lincoln County. According to most of those who tell this story, the ship was commanded by Spanish pirates, fresh from several successful raids on trading vessels and merchant ships along the California coast to the south.

Watching the arrival of the pirate ship were the residents of a small Indian village located just beyond the shore. During the next few days, the watchers observed the pirates making repairs on the hull of the vessel. Presently, rowboats carrying several of the seamen arrived at the village, and after being led to fresh-water springs by the Indians, they filled their water barrels and returned to the ship. Soon, the Indians were providing fresh meat to the pirates in exchange for blankets, tools, and beads.

As the days passed, the vessel continued to take on water and soon began listing to one side as the efforts to control the leak were unsuccessful. When it became certain that the ship would surely sink to the bottom of the bay, the pirates loaded a large wooden chest filled with gold coins and jewelry into one of the rowboats and transported it to shore. Three other rowboats followed, and eventually about twenty sailors landed on the nearby shore.

The leader of the pirates, a tall, bearded sailor wearing a long, crimson cape, directed his followers to a particular location on the shore and ordered them to excavate a hole in which to bury the chest. As the men began shoveling dirt aside, they were approached by several elders of the Indian tribe who informed them they were digging into a sacred burial ground and asked them to cease. Unmoved by the Indians' request, the pirate captain ordered several of his men to chase the elders from the area. At the point of swords and muskets, the Indians were herded back to their village.

When the chest was finally buried, the captain appointed two men to stand guard over it lest the Indians return and attempt to dig it up. One of the guards was a man of slight build and long mustaches that extended below his chin. Though somewhat frail looking, this pirate carried a long sword, which he pulled from his belt from time to time and with which he engaged in mock fights with an imaginary opponent. The other guard was a huge black man, well-muscled, and standing close to seven feet in height. The black man was believed to have been a mute, for he never uttered a word. He remained expressionless save those times when his smaller companion jabbed at him with his sword, pestering him with feints and simulated jousting.

Two days later, the pirate vessel sank. Just before going under the waters of the bay, the sailors removed several trunkloads of goods and carried them to shore. After making several rowboat trips from the ship to shore, the entire complement of pirates finally stood on the beach awaiting orders from the captain.

The captain learned from the Indians that other white men were believed to be living among other tribes several miles inland. In the hope of making contact with the whites and obtaining overland directions back to Mexico, the captain led his followers across the dunes and into the woods beyond. Before leaving, he informed the two men guarding the treasure they were to remain until summoned by a runner.

A week passed, and the two men faithfully watched over the buried fortune in gold and jewels. With each day, however, the large black man grew more and more annoyed with the antics of the smaller one. On several occasions, the latter, brandishing his sword, jabbed violently at the black man, drawing trickles of blood from the resulting wounds. Unable to tolerate the stabbings any longer, the black man, enraged, seized his companion, and rained several mighty blows onto his skull, crushing it and killing the sailor instantly. Excavating a shallow hole in the sand atop the treasure chest, the black man buried the dead sailor.

Several Indians were watching when the black man killed his companion, and they quickly ran back to the village and informed the leaders. Following a brief council, it was decided that the tribe could no longer tolerate the desecration of their burial ground at the hands of the newcomers, and they decided to demand the remaining guard leave the area.

The next morning, a contingent of armed warriors approached the large black guard and, using sign, ordered him away. When he refused to move, one of the Indians hurled a lance at the feet of the guard. Seizing the lance, he pulled it from the ground and broke it in half across his knee. Grabbing the nearest Indian, he snapped his neck with powerful hands and threw the dead man aside.

Almost immediately, a rain of arrows and lances fell upon the black man and, seriously wounded, he collapsed to the ground. Seconds later, the warriors were upon him, kicking him and beating his head and torso with clubs until he too was eventually killed. After mutilating the body and breaking the limb bones, the Indians buried the black man beside the body of his smaller companion.

Days later, the entire tribe, believing the beach was cursed and that bad luck had surely befallen them, loaded up their belongings and departed, eventually resettling on a coastal location several dozen miles to the north. On the abandoned beach they had quit, there remained little evidence that it had ever been occupied save the three or four middens, or shell mounds, and the graveyard. During the coming winters, violent storms sweeping in from the Pacific Oceans would obliterate even those.

At the beginning of the twentieth century, the Oregon coast began to draw tourists by the thousands. The pleasant sandy beaches located among the picturesque rocky headlands became a favorite for those who liked to picnic and swim in the surf.

E.G. Calkins, a businessman and resident of Lincoln County, owned a stretch of shoreline that included Three Rocks Beach. Calkins, who sometimes fished in the bay with nets, once brought up some wooden remains of a vessel that had apparently sunk long before. On days when the water was clear, Calkins claimed one could see the outline of the sunken ship lying on the bottom sands. Calkins claimed the ship was once a sailing vessel and was almost 150 feet long.

Convinced he could make some money providing camping sites and facilities to tourists, Calkins arranged to have a portion of the beach leveled. Using a large plow pulled by a team of mules, Calkins and his workers broke up many of the humps and hillocks and, using a scraper, smoothed out much of the area. From time to time, Calkins' plow would break into a midden and expose some artifacts. The businessman, always fascinated by such things, would stop to examine them, often collecting interesting pieces. From the middens, Calkins retrieved arrowheads, broken pottery, an occasional axe head, and other remnants of a bygone culture. During the course of leveling the beach, he had accumulated three or four buckets full of such things.

During the spring of 1931, Calkins was breaking up a section of the beach that had grown up in seagrass when his plowing exposed some bones. One of the men he had hired to follow him with the scraper stopped to examine one of the bones and pronounced it human. After digging around in the sand for another half hour, the two men eventually excavated the skeletal remains of two human beings.

One of the skeletons astounded Calkins and the hired man: the large, thick bones were the remains of a man at least seven feet tall! Most of the leg and arm bones of the larger man had been broken, and the skulls of both were crushed. While plowing nearby, Calkins unearthed nearly a dozen more skeletons during the next two weeks.

Curious about his find, Calkins sought the expertise of two friends—Dr. John Horner and Dr. F.M. Carter. Horner was a well-known scholar who specialized in Oregon history, and Carter was a skilled physician who knew a great deal about West Coast Indians. Most of the skeletons uncovered during Calkins' leveling activities, according to Carter, belonged to Indians, and were probably interred in a burial ground. After reconstructing the largest skeleton, Carter, after examining it closely, determined that it had belonged to a Negro. The nature of the broken bones suggested he may have been tortured or beaten just prior to death.

Several weeks passed, and eventually the discovery of the huge skeleton was reported in the area newspapers. More time went by, and one morning an old Indian appeared at the home of Calkins, requesting an audience with the businessman. While Calkins listened intently, the old man related an Indian legend about a strange ship arriving in the bay at Three Rocks Beach, the burial of a treasure chest, the killing of a black giant, and his subsequent burial atop the gold.

Calkins grew quite interested when the Indian mentioned treasure, and when the old man finally left, he returned to the beach with the intention of digging deeper into the ground where the huge skeleton was found.

When Calkins arrived at the beach, however, he realized he had done his job too well. The area had been completely leveled, and every place looked the same. Several holes were excavated with the help of his workers, but nothing was ever found.

Today, the large wooden pirate chest filled with gold and jewels still rests under several feet of sand somewhere on Three Rocks Beach.

Mount Mazama Gold

Yreka, California, is located only about twenty miles south of the Oregon border in Siskiyou County. During the month of February in the year 1850, one of the coldest winters ever to descend on this region struck the area, making travel to and from the nearby gold mines difficult, if not impossible. As a result, most of the miners and prospectors contented themselves with drinking and playing games of chance in Yreka's local taverns, of which there were several.

One evening an old miner, name unknown, rode into Yreka leading a heavily laden packhorse. Having just completed a treacherous week negotiating the snow- and ice-clogged passes in the mountains north of town, he looked forward to relaxing in the warmth of a friendly tavern. After making arrangements to leave his horses in a livery for the night, the man, close to sixty years old, shouldered a pair of heavy saddlebags and walked to the nearest tavern.

Stepping up to the bar, the whiskered old miner dumped several handfuls of gold nuggets onto the smooth, varnished oak surface and told the bartender to set up drinks for everybody. Within seconds, two dozen men had crowded around the newcomer, gaping at the size and quality of the shiny nuggets that lay before them.

Throughout the night, the old man bought drinks for the full house and swapped tales of panning and prospecting for gold in the Cascade Range of California and Oregon.

Eventually, the talk got around to the location of the old man's gold mine. His response to the many questions was good-natured and friendly, but the newcomer remained evasive about specific locations and landmarks and told the questioners only that the source of his gold was a placer mine located about seventy-five miles to the north in the Oregon wilderness. Near the mine, he said, he had constructed a small log cabin.

The old miner remained in Yreka for several days until the weather cleared and some of the snow and ice melted, making travel through the passes safer. While staying in town, he purchased provisions for another journey to his placer mine. He spent his days caring for his animals and packing up his fresh provisions. He spent his evenings at the local taverns, where he continued to buy drinks for any and all who entered.

Two days before departing Yreka, the old man confided the location of his mine to a man named Wilson with whom he had become quite friendly. "If anything ever happens to me," he told his new companion, "you are free to travel to the mine and pan the gold for yourself." Bidding Wilson goodbye, the old miner, leading his packhorse, rode north out of town toward the mountains in Oregon.

The following February, the miner returned to Yreka where he once again regularly purchased drinks for the miners who were wintering in the area, always paying with gold nuggets. The old man spent a great deal of time visiting with his friend, and showed him several samples of gold ore which he had taken from the mine. The gold, the old man claimed, was very plentiful and of an extremely high quality.

The following year, 1852, the old man failed to show up in Yreka. Many presumed he was simply busy with his gold mine and didn't have time to spare, but, as the days turned into weeks, his friend Wilson became concerned.

Around the first week of April, Wilson was convinced that tragedy had befallen the old man and, using the directions given to him, decided to try to find the mine. Wilson gathered a party of ten men, all of them well known to him and with mining experience. Using the directions provided by the old miner, the group set out for the Oregon wilderness.

After three days of travel on horseback, the party arrived at Jacksonville, a small settlement in what is now Jackson County, Oregon. Gold had been discovered in Jackson Creek a few months earlier, and the population of the town swelled to nearly ten thousand. Miners were living in tents, shanties—anywhere they could locate shelter.

Wilson's party decided to remain in Jacksonville for two days, resting the horses and stocking up on provisions for the long trip into the mountains. After setting up camp on the outskirts of town, several of the men decided to ride into the settlement and have a few beers. While drinking and playing cards with some of the local citizens, one of Wilson's companions let it slip that they were traveling north in search of a very rich gold mine. One of the card players, a miner named Hillman, asked several questions about the mine and its location. Hillman was soon convinced of the potential richness of the mine, and decided to assemble a group of men to follow the Wilson party.

When Wilson led his men out of Jacksonville and toward the Cascade Range to the northeast, Hillman, accompanied by six of his friends, followed at a distance of several hundred yards. It soon became clear to Wilson that he was being followed. He tried to lose the Hillman party several times but was unsuccessful. After several days of traveling, the Wilson and Hillman parties eventually wound up sharing the same campsites each evening.

The two groups, deciding to combine their efforts, finally arrived at the base of Mount Mazama in the Cascade Range. Using the information provided by the old miner,

Wilson, Hillman, and several others set out in search of the gold mine. The directions, however, proved quite confusing. At a point where the trail forked, Wilson led two of his men in one direction while Hillman and several of his followers took the opposite one.

Hours later, Wilson crested a ridge and looked down into the clear waters of what eventually became known as Crater Lake. At this point, he realized he had taken the wrong turn, and returned back down the trail.

In the meantime, Hillman's group split up and each man rode in a different direction searching for the mine. About two hours later, Hillman spotted one of his companions returning along a narrow hillside trail, waving frantically.

As Hillman rode toward him, the fellow yelled that he had discovered a tiny log cabin near a stream flowing through a shallow canyon. As the rider turned his horse to return back down the trail, the animal lost its footing. Seconds later, horse and rider were tumbling together down the steep slope into the canyon bottom hundreds of feet below. Both were killed instantly.

Later that same day, a party comprised of Wilson, Hillman, and a few of their followers tried to retrace the path taken by the dead rider. Though they searched for several days, they were never able to locate the stream or the cabin. Eventually, they left the mountain and returned to their homes.

The story of the old man's gold mine, a rich placer deposit located near a log cabin, circulated throughout northern California and southern Oregon for years. From time to time, men would arrive at Mount Mazama to search for the wealth they knew lay somewhere nearby, but if anyone ever found it, it was never announced.

Today, the huge, clear blue-water lake Wilson observed is known as Crater Lake and is a National Park. Somewhere along the slopes near the base of the mountain lies a long-lost rich placer mine.

The Lost Log Cabin Placer

While the War Between the States was raging far to the south and east, the Pacific Northwest remained a healthy, growing region of the country, seemingly untroubled by the violent conflict and political disagreement manifested by the Union and the Confederacy.

Fishing, logging, trapping, and trade prospered throughout Washington, Oregon, and northern California. Even though many years had passed since the boom times of the colorful and exciting Gold Rush days, prospecting and mining remained viable for the persistent and hard-working outdoorsmen willing to brave the oft-inclement weather and sometimes dangerous Indians.

Two such men were a pair of Frenchmen who appeared in what is now the city of Eugene, Oregon, in 1863. Though unable to speak English, the two, believed to be brothers, purchased several weeks' worth of supplies and mining equipment at a hardware store in Klamath Falls, Oregon, to outfit themselves for a placer mining expedition somewhere along a tributary to the Willamette River.

As the store clerk totaled up the charges for the equipment, he watched wide-eyed and curious as they carefully counted out several nuggets of shiny gold. Using sign language throughout most of the transaction, the clerk inquired about the origin of such fine-looking gold. Hand-signing a response, one of the Frenchmen described a small canyon not many days to the southeast. The canyon contained a shallow stream rich in placer gold, a stream that apparently was a tributary to the Willamette River. Being somewhat familiar with the region described by the Frenchman, the clerk recognized the area as what the locals called Coal Creek.

The Frenchmen rode out of town the following morning, leading two packhorses loaded with equipment. Two months later they returned for more supplies. Their first stop, however, was the bank, where they made a deposit of nearly $50,000 in gold nuggets, nuggets they explained came from their productive placer mine. The bank in which they left their hard-earned gold was not one in the formal sense, but merely a small room located in the rear of the hardware store where the proprietor charged a small fee for guarding over such deposits.

After spending several days in Eugene, the Frenchmen gathered up their remaining gold, of which they had plenty, and traveled to San Francisco, where they spent the winter living luxuriously in a fine hotel, eating sumptuous meals, and drinking fine wine—imported from France, naturally.

By the time spring arrived, the Frenchmen had exhausted their wealth and decided to return to their placer diggings in Oregon. Purchasing a pair of horses, they made the journey from San Francisco northward, arriving at an Indian campground near Klamath Falls around the time the snow was beginning to melt from the higher mountain passes.

After spending approximately a week at Klamath Falls, the Frenchmen departed for their diggings. In tow, however, was an Indian woman they brought along to handle the cooking and cleaning chores. On arriving at the diggings several days later, the Frenchmen returned to their panning while the Indian woman busied herself with maintaining the camp.

Two months later, the same Indian woman wandered, exhausted, into a camp of soldiers near present-day Lowell. She had been badly beaten and her clothes were torn to shreds. She told the soldiers an incredible tale of being held as a slave by the two miners, who often beat and abused her. She told the leader of the party, Captain F.B. Sprague, that, fearing for her life, she fled from the camp of the Frenchmen, became lost in the woods, and had not eaten in several days.

When Sprague asked directions to the miners' camp, the Indian woman was unable to provide precise details, but she said they lived in a low, three-sided log cabin built against the exposed wall of a natural rock outcrop. The gold diggings, she said, were a short distance from the cabin, and across the stream was a wide meadow where the miners pastured their horses.

Sprague, along with his contingent of troops, searched for the Frenchmen's camp for several days but was unable to locate it. The Indian woman eventually made her way back to her people near Klamath Falls, and when she explained her plight to her family, her brother, a warrior of some note, vowed revenge on the miners.

Leading a group of some twelve armed braves, the brother searched for the camp of the Frenchmen for several weeks. Each of the accompanying warriors was a true fighting man and had proven personal valor and courage in previous battles. Eventually, they found the miners' log cabin.

Lying in wait in the nearby forest, the Indians waited for the two men to return from their diggings, and when they did they attacked and killed them.

After dragging the bodies of the dead men into the cabin, the Indians discovered a huge gold cache consisting of several canvas bags filled with placer gold and piled into one corner of the dwelling. When one of the braves lifted a bag, the leader warned him that to possess the wealth of the white men was to bring bad luck upon the tribe. The Indian returned the ore sack to the pile and the warriors soon departed, returning to Klamath Falls.

For years, the Indians boasted of tracking and killing the two Frenchmen and finding the store of placer gold in the cabin. The story circulated around the Indian encampment near Klamath Falls and was often heard by visiting white men. Several of the white men attempted to hire the Indians who slew the Frenchmen as guides to the log cabin and the wealth contained therein, but all refused for fear of cursing the tribe forever.

Numerous attempts have been made during the past hundred years to locate the curious three-sided log cabin near the rich placer stream, but all have failed. According to researchers, the diggings are believed to be located within a twenty-mile radius of Illahe Peak in the Umpqua National Forest. Others say that site is too far south and locate the placer mine closer to Bohemia Mountain in Lane County. Still others place it near Holland Peak close to present-day Oakridge.

Wherever the lost log-cabin mine is located, it is certain to yield incredible wealth in the form of rich and plentiful placer gold.

The Lost Hermit Treasure

Among the oddest tales of lost treasure ever to come out of the Pacific Northwest is that related to a desperate stagecoach robbery, a case of mistaken identity, a hermit, and a fortune in gold and cash, a treasure that remains lost to this day.

The town of Boise City, Idaho (now just called Boise), was a rapidly growing and fairly prosperous community in the years immediately following the Civil War. Hundreds of miners who dug and panned the ore from the rock outcrops and streams of the nearby mountains often arrived at this outpost of civilization to purchase supplies and patronize the numerous taverns and brothels. Businessmen and speculators perceived boom times ahead for this somewhat remote Western town and anticipated huge profits. As a result, retail stores proliferated and various businesses such as saloons, law offices, real estate operations, hotels, liveries, blacksmith shops, and banks abounded. Schools, churches, newspapers, and even opera houses soon followed.

During the summer of 1865, a down-and-out placer miner named Pickett spent much of his time hanging around Boise City. Between occasional day work as a handyman and seeking handouts from passersby, he was able to eke out a precarious survival. Pickett was generally a loner with very few friends. He had spent much of the previous eighteen months deep in the mountains northeast of Boise City in search of a strike, but was only able to pan enough gold to barely keep himself supplied and fed.

While in Boise City, Pickett slept under the wooden loading dock of the Wells Fargo Company. One morning just after dawn, Pickett was awakened by a conversation taking place above him on the platform, a conversation that was to change his life forever. Pickett listened intently as a Wells Fargo official and the dock foreman were discussing an outgoing shipment consisting of two metal chests containing several gold bars and an unspecified amount of cash. As Pickett lay quietly on the ground beneath the dock, he overheard the official mention that the shipment was to leave that afternoon for the tiny community of Owyhee to the south.

Pickett, deciding that robbery might be easier and considerably more profitable than placer mining, determined then and there to steal the shipment.

Stealing two horses from a nearby corral, Pickett traveled south from Boise City along the road the stage would follow. After riding for several miles, he eventually arrived at a point along the road where a steep grade commenced. Knowing that the speed of the wagon would be slowed considerably while negotiating the hill, Pickett hid in a grove of trees near the top and waited.

About two hours past noon, Pickett heard the distant creak and rattle of a wagon and its traces. Peering from his hiding place, he discerned the approaching Wells Fargo wagon. Pickett knew that among the cargo lashed down in the back of the wagon were the two metal chests containing gold and cash, a small fortune that would soon be his.

Perched upon the spring seat of the wagon were the driver and a guard. As the driver lashed at the four stout horses who pulled the wagon, the guard tried to sleep away the effects of the previous night's drinking. From his hiding place, Pickett noticed that the guard's shotgun lay at his feet in the bottom of the wagon.

When the wagon was about twenty yards from the top of the grade, Pickett levered a shell into his rifle and spurred his mount out into the road in front of the wagon. As the surprised driver pulled up on the reins and brought the vehicle to a stop, the guard snapped awake. Pickett immediately ordered the two men to throw their guns to the ground and unload the shipment. At Pickett's insistence, the driver, using an axe, broke open the locks on the metal chests containing the gold and money.

After tying up the two men, Pickett loaded about two hundred pounds of gold bars and all of the cash onto the spare horse and rode away toward the northwest.

The next day, a small wagon train of immigrants riding toward Boise City from the south found the two Wells Fargo employees lying by the side of the road, still bound. On being freed, the men drove the wagon back to Boise City and reported the brazen theft to their employer. The next day, lawmen and Wells Fargo detectives rode to the robbery site and looked for the tracks of the bandit, but a heavy rain from the previous evening had obliterated any useful sign.

Pickett, keeping mainly to seldom-used trails and remote, unpopulated sections of the country, traveled horseback for several days through eastern Oregon. Stopping only occasionally to feed and water his horses, the robber made good time and eventually arrived at The Dalles on the Columbia River, where he rented a hotel room for several weeks and kept his stolen fortune hidden under the bed.

Meanwhile, a man named Higgins, Pickett's former placer mining partner, was arrested in Boise City for the robbery of the Wells Fargo shipment. Higgins, who was of the same height and general appearance as Pickett and who even wore the same kind of overalls and red flannel shirt, was mistakenly identified by the Wells Fargo driver and guard as the man who had robbed them and tied them up.

Weeks later, Pickett read about the arrest in a newspaper he purchased in The Dalles. Surprised, and suddenly infused with a strong feeling of guilt, he considered returning to Boise City, giving back the stolen loot, and confessing to the robbery so his friend could go free. Pickett considered this notion for several days, but eventually decided that the courts would soon realize they had arrested the wrong man and eventually set him free.

It was not to be the case. About a month later, Pickett was shocked to read that his partner had been convicted of the crime and sentenced to a dozen years in the Idaho State Penitentiary. Though burdened with a heavy guilt, Pickett realized he lacked the courage to return to Idaho. Instead, he gathered up his gold and money, loaded it onto a packhorse, and fled to the solitude of the Cascade Range, located just southwest of The Dalles. In the shadow of the prominence of Mount Hood, Pickett constructed a crude log cabin and pursued the life of a hermit for many years. Depending almost entirely on wild game for sustenance, Pickett rarely came into town.

About eight years later, Pickett, his face now deeply lined, his body stooped, and his system racked with continuous deep coughing, finally decided to return to Boise City to confess his crime. Since he did not own a packhorse now, Pickett buried the stolen goods in a location near his cabin. This done, he undertook the long journey back to Idaho.

Upon arriving in the bustling, thriving town, Pickett immediately fell ill and was carried to the office of a local physician. After examining him thoroughly, the doctor told Pickett he was suffering from consumption and likely had only a few days to live. As the guilt-ridden man lay on a flimsy cot in the physician's quarters, he wrote a lengthy statement confessing to the robbery of the Wells Fargo shipment eight years earlier. In the note, Pickett described his humble cabin near Mount Hood and provided directions for finding it, even drawing a crude map. He also related how he had buried the stolen gold and money at the base of a thick tree stump not far from the front door of his cabin.

The following day, Pickett died.

On the basis of Pickett's written confession, Higgins was released from prison a few days later. After receiving the directions to the buried loot, Wells Fargo agents traveled to The Dalles, and then into the rugged Cascade Range. Though they searched for days for Pickett's cabin, they had no luck whatsoever and, after about three weeks of combing the region, gave up and returned to Idaho.

Others have entered the Cascade Range in search of Pickett's gold over the years only to meet with similar results.

In October 1957, a group of deer hunters arrived in the Cascades for an annual hunt. While hiking up a small, remote canyon on the north slope of Mount Hood in search of deer signs, they found a very old, poorly constructed, partially fallen-down log cabin. The four hunters camped near the cabin for three days, ranging out every morning in various directions in search of game. The cabin, according to the hunters, had apparently been abandoned for decades.

On returning to their homes in The Dalles, the hunters told some people about their recent trip and the old cabin they found, only to learn from a few old-timers that the structure near which they camped was likely the habitat of Pickett. When the old-timers told the story of the buried gold and money, the four men organized a second expedition into the region.

Though they searched for three days, the men were unable to relocate the cabin.

During the mid-1860s, two hundred pounds of gold would have been worth several thousand dollars. Today, it, along with the cash, would be valued at closer to $100,000—perhaps considerably more, depending on the collector value.

And as far as anyone knows, the valuable cache is still there, buried next to an old tree stump in some remote valley located on the north drainage of Mount Hood.

Deathbed Confession Discloses Cache of Gold

During the autumn of 1942, an elderly man who gave his name as Alton Baker lay dying in a hospital ward in Eugene, Oregon. Though ravaged by old age and its accompanying infirmities, it was obvious the old man had been hale and robust in his younger days and had apparently led a life in the out-of-doors. One of the attending nurses stated that he "looked like a man with a history and not all of it good." The old fellow said little about himself and spoke seldom, usually to inquire about when he might be able to leave the hospital.

It was not to happen. The doctors told Baker he would die soon and that nothing could be done about it. Several days after he received this information, the old man, with a look of haunted desperation in his eyes, grabbed the shirttail of a young male hospital orderly and asked him to sit down and listen to a story. During the next hour, as the patient young man sat by the bedside of the dying Baker, he heard an incredible tale of a hidden fortune and the bizarre circumstances that surrounded it.

During the 1870s, Alton Baker prowled the trails leading into and out of Grants Pass, Oregon, and earned his living by robbing stagecoaches and travelers. In the company of two fellow outlaws, he preyed on the weak, the unarmed, and the unsuspecting—and eventually amassed an impressive horde of gold and cash.

One day, Baker and his companions learned about a large gold shipment as it was passing through the town of Woodville (now Rogue River) and heading for San Francisco. Taking along three packhorses, the outlaws waited at a location along the trail and stopped the coach as it approached. After tying up the driver and guard, they broke open the large chests carrying the gold and transferred the shipment into saddlebags, which they lashed to their own horses as well as the extra mounts. Riding away from the scene of the crime, the three bandits covered several miles before turning into the drainage basin of Foots Creek, a location they had settled on days earlier. Once deep into the Foots Creek valley, the riders stopped at the entrance to an old mine tunnel into which they cached the gold.

That evening, while finishing dinner around the campfire, the three men entered into a discussion related to the division of the loot. Unhappy with his share, one of the bandits drew a pistol from beneath his blanket and was immediately shot dead by the other two men. As the mortally wounded outlaw drew his final breaths, Baker pointed his pistol at the remaining partner and killed him on the spot. As Baker related this part of the story to the orderly, tears welled up in his aged eyes and he wondered aloud how he could ever be forgiven for such a greedy and cowardly act.

In the light of the full moon that dominated the canyon of Foots Creek that night, Baker dragged the two dead men into the old mine shaft and, after several tiring trips, removed the gold to a different location—the base of an old madroña tree. Here he buried the loot in a deep hole he scooped out of the ground near the trunk, finished the chore just minutes before sunrise.

When the morning sun finally illuminated the shallow canyon, Baker broke camp, packed his gear onto his horse, and prepared to leave. He intended to return in a year when the threat of pursuit by lawmen had diminished. After turning the other horses loose, he regarded the madroña tree next to his gold cache. Since it looked like several others growing in this part of the canyon, the outlaw decided to mark it somehow. Casting about the campsite, he found a broken saddle horn, which he wedged into a fork of the tree before riding away toward California.

As the outlaw passed the time in Sacramento, he fell into a habit of taking drinks each evening at an establishment called the Glitter Tavern. One night, he entered into an argument with a fellow patron and, during an ensuing scuffle, stabbed him to death. Baker was arrested, tried, convicted, and sentenced to life in the state prison.

As Baker languished in the penitentiary, his dreams were often filled with visions of the fortune in gold cached at the base of the madroña tree in faraway Foots Creek canyon. At times, the images of his dead partners would intrude during his sleep and he would awaken screaming.

Many years passed, and Baker, a model prisoner, was eventually paroled. Penniless, he was forced to seek employment and soon found a job working on a freight dock. More time passed while Baker patiently and gradually saved his money until such time as he could purchase a horse and supplies and depart for the Foots Creek area in Oregon.

As Baker labored on the loading docks, he was occasionally seized by a severe and unrelenting cough. During a visit to a physician one afternoon, he learned he was suffering from tuberculosis, an ailment he likely picked up while in prison.

Sometimes Baker's coughing spells were so bad he had to be carried to the hospital, and over time the money he saved for his return trip to Oregon was gradually used up on doctors and hospital costs.

More time passed, months graded into years, and Baker was finally able to save enough money to make the trip to Oregon. The year was 1931, and, driving a used Model-A

Ford, the former outlaw, now past eighty, anxiously drove the long, winding roads into southwestern Oregon.

When he arrived in the region he knew so well as a young man, he was amazed at how much change had occurred. Settlements had sprung up where once only wilderness could be found. Time and again, Baker had to retrace his route in search of Foots Creek, for new roads and trails, extensive logging, and large new farms and ranches in the area left him confused.

Finally Baker found the entrance to the canyon, and where the road ended he spotted a cabin set near the bank of the stream. Exiting his automobile, Baker approached the cabin and was greeted by the residents—a married couple named Prefontaine. Politely, he asked for permission to leave his vehicle parked nearby while he explored the canyon. The Prefontaines welcomed the newcomer to do so and even invited him to stop and visit with them on his return.

Several hours later, a tired and troubled Baker walked out of the canyon and knocked on the door of the Prefontaine cabin. Though he shared dinner with the couple and remained to visit for a short time afterward, the old outlaw was decidedly uncommunicative and appeared nervous and distracted. Finally, after thanking his hosts, he climbed into the car and drove away.

Just before he died in the lonely hospital ward, Alton Baker told the orderly that, on arriving at the location where he had buried the gold near the madroña tree, he recalled his participation in the deaths of his partners and a painful feeling of guilt and remorse overcame him. Associating the long-buried stagecoach loot with something evil, Baker grew frightened and hastened out of the canyon. Before leaving, however, he searched for and found the old wooden saddle horn still wedged in the fork of the madroña tree that shaded the site of the cached stagecoach loot.

Baker was buried in a pauper's cemetery. Approximately three months following the death of the old man, the orderly, in the company of his wife, drove to Foots Creek in the hope of locating the buried treasure. The year was 1942 and, using the directions provided by the old outlaw on his deathbed, the couple drove up to the Prefontaine residence.

After chatting with the Prefontaines for nearly an hour, the orderly finally explained the reason for his visit, relating in detail Alton Baker's deathbed confession to his part in the robbery and the killing of his partners. The Prefontaines remembered Baker well from his earlier visit and were intrigued by the tale of buried treasure.

After pondering this incredible tale for several minutes, Mr. Prefontaine told the orderly that he had been in the Foots Creek canyon on several occasions and knew exactly where the old mine shaft was located. Furthermore, he stated, he recalled once encountering an old madroña tree with a busted saddle horn wedged into a fork about chest-high! Moments later, the two men were hiking up the canyon, eager to find the long-lost cache of gold.

Prefontaine had no trouble whatsoever locating the old mine tunnel and led the orderly straight to it, but since his last visit to this area years earlier, most of it had caved in.

Several yards away, at the foot of the gentle slope extending from the opening to the mine, lay a grove of madroña trees. Though the two men searched among the trees for over an hour, they could find not a single one containing a broken saddle horn. Prefontaine ventured the opinion that the old wooden horn had simply rotted away and fallen from its perch.

Discouraged, the two men returned to the cabin and around sundown the orderly and his wife drove away, never to return. Prefontaine, however, was intrigued by the story of the buried stagecoach loot and returned to the madroña grove many times over the next few years in the hope of finding some clue as to which tree grew next to the cache. Though he excavated several promising locations, he found nothing.

Eventually, Prefontaine tired of the search and gave up hope of ever locating the buried treasure. During the 1950s, however, he read a magazine article that introduced him to metal detectors and he decided one of these machines had the potential to locate the lost gold. Prefontaine purchased one of the instruments from a mail-order catalog. After it was delivered, he familiarized himself with its operation, and, with great anticipation, carried it into the canyon to the grove of trees.

On arriving, Prefontaine was surprised and disappointed to discover that a fire had ravaged the madroña grove, burning it away entirely. Furthermore, and equally discouraging, a subsequent flood had covered much of the area with a deposit of stream gravel. Using his new machine, Prefontaine scanned the ground where he believed the madroña grove to have been, but he received no positive signal whatsoever.

Discouraged once again, Prefontaine gave up the search for good. Since he was now elderly and in failing health, it was the last time he was ever to visit the canyon.

Estimates of the value of the gold buried by Alton Baker in the Foots Creek canyon range from $20,000 to $150,000 in 1870s values. If found, this remarkable cache would be worth a sizable fortune today.

Secret Gold Mine of the Chinook Indians

Much of Oregon's Pacific Coast is characterized by high cliffs and rugged, rocky shores. As a result, coastal regions possessing calm bays and gently sloping beaches were prized among those who first sought to settle in the region. A decent port led to oceanic commerce, and for more than two hundred years, trading ships and merchant vessels have been observed plying the waters up and down the coast, hauling goods to and from populated areas.

One particularly prized Oregon harbor was Tillamook Bay in Tillamook County, located in the northwestern part of the state. The calm and protected waters of the bay afforded a choice anchor for sailing ships, and the gentle coastline, accompanied by the broad fertile valley of the Trask River, afforded agricultural opportunities for the many who chose to locate in the region.

White settlement around Tillamook Bay dates back to the time of the fur trappers. Many of them, hardy mountain men all, would transport loads of beaver pelts from the trapping grounds of the inland Coast and Cascade Ranges to the bay and await the arrival of ships that would carry the cargo to the markets along the East Coast.

Before white men discovered this area, the Chinook Indians found Tillamook Bay much to their liking. Fish and shellfish were plentiful, and wild game was abundant in the nearby forests. The Chinook were a relatively friendly tribe and they enthusiastically welcomed the trappers to their camps. Some of the mountain men took Chinook wives and remained in the area to settle and raise families.

The first trappers to frequent this region heard stories of a secret gold mine that was sometimes visited by the Chinook. Occasionally, a few of the men would make the two- to three-day journey to a remote part of the Coast Range to retrieve gold ore, which they used for fashioning bracelets and other jewelry. Those few white men who had an opportunity to examine the gold brought in by the Indians maintained it was of the purest quality and claimed a piece carved directly from the rock matrix could easily be hammered into the shape of an ornament. The trappers often asked the Indians about the location of the gold mine, but such questions were always met with silence.

As more and more trappers came to the region, and as the bay was frequented by an increasing number of sailing vessels, word of the secret Chinook gold mine spread among them. Once the Indians perceived the value white men placed on the yellow ore, they visited the mine more frequently and returned with enough to trade for blankets, tools, and weapons. The whites continued to ask about the mine's location, but the Chinook were adamant in their refusal to reveal it.

Years passed, and this northwestern portion of Oregon grew more and more settled as newly arriving immigrants discovered grand opportunities for ranching, farming, and trading in the area. Before long, the town of Portland was founded some seventy miles east of the coast, on the opposite side of the Coast Range. The city was located where an important trade route intersected with the Columbia River, and soon it evolved into a vital and thriving financial center.

As white civilization encroached on the region, the traditional Indian ways of living changed rapidly and dramatically. Seldom did the Chinook fish the oceans and hunt game in the mountains any more; instead, they traveled to the cities and towns of the white men and purchased goods at their stores. And they often paid with gold nuggets taken from their secret mine.

On several occasions, Chinook Indians traveling on foot from the Coast Range would arrive at a store in Gales City, located just west of Portland. Here they purchased food and clothing, all paid for with nearly pure gold nuggets. The storekeeper repeatedly asked the Indians where they obtained the ore, but his only response was silence. As a result of the merchant's continued questioning and pressure, the Chinook took their business to nearby Forest Grove and a mercantile owned by one T.H. Cornelius. As before, the Indians always paid for their purchases with gold nuggets.

Cornelius, happy for the business provided by the Indians, was also eager to learn the source of the gold, but after a few initial inquiries he detected their resistance and never asked again.

One afternoon, a group of five drifters was hanging around Cornelius's mercantile when three Chinook Indians arrived. After watching the Indians—one old man and two young boys—pay for their goods with impressively large gold nuggets, the men decided to follow them as they lugged their heavy bundles westward into the mountains.

About four miles from the store, the three men overtook the Indians and demanded they reveal the source of their gold. Steadfastly, the Chinook refused to speak. One of the drifters dismounted and pistol-whipped the oldest of the three Indians, but still they would not speak.

After threatening to shoot one of the boys in the head, the old one spoke up and, in a weak and halting voice, told the man that no Indian would ever betray the tribe by revealing the location of the secret gold mine. Death, he informed the attackers, was preferable to disloyalty.

Frustrated, the men mounted up and rode away.

As word of the Indians' gold spread throughout the region, enterprising prospectors and treasure hunters ventured into the area to try to find the mine. It was generally believed that the secret mine was located deep in the Coast Range somewhere between Tillamook Bay and Portland.

One evening at dusk, in the eastern foothills of the Coast Range, four prospectors were seated around a campfire finishing their meal when they spotted two Chinook Indians walking along the trail some fifty yards away, both transporting heavy loads. Curious as to what the Indians were carrying, the prospectors overtook them and demanded they open their packs. The Indians, a father and his son, did so, and the four miners stood in awe as they gazed upon the contents—nearly sixty pounds of gold nuggets!

Immediately, the prospectors demanded to know where the gold came from, but the Indians refused to speak. After nearly two hours of threats and torture, the Chinook maintained their silence. Finally, in a fit of anger and frustration, one of the prospectors drew his pistol and shot and killed both Indians.

For years the Chinook had been growing uncomfortable with the increasing pressure placed on them by outsiders to reveal the location of their secret gold mine. Now, with the death of two tribal members, they began to think the mine was cursed, and that to continue to take gold from it would further anger the spirits they believed dwelt within. At that point, the tribal leaders decided no one should ever remove gold from the mine again. The next morning, eight men were sent to the mine to conceal it so that none would ever find it. Other tribal members were cautioned never to speak of the mine or reveal the location.

Sometime during the first decade of the twentieth century, a family named White farmed a large portion of the Trask River floodplain near Tillamook Bay. Two generations of the Whites cooperated in this endeavor and shared a housekeeper, a Chinook Indian woman they called Mae. Though in her seventies, Mae worked six days a week cleaning houses and cooking for the two large families.

One cold, dreary winter morning, Mae developed a high fever and, though she tried to work, eventually collapsed and remained unconscious for several hours. After examining her, the community physician told the Whites that Mae was seriously ill and had only a few weeks to live.

Day and night, members of the White family remained at the bedside of the old woman, constantly bathing her head with cool towels and seeing to her every need. While family members hoped and prayed the faithful housekeeper would recover, it grew apparent they would lose her.

Ruby White was the youngest member of the White family, and more than any of the others she sat by Mae's bedside watching over the old woman. Mae had practically raised Ruby from an infant, taught her the songs and stories of the Chinook people, and saw her grow into a beautiful young woman. Ruby loved Mae almost as much as she did her own mother, and the kind Indian woman dearly loved the young girl.

Late one evening, Ruby sat alone with Mae after the rest of the family had gone to bed. Caressing the rough, calloused brown hand of the old woman, Ruby bowed her head and silently mouthed prayers that Mae would have a safe and peaceful voyage to heaven. When Ruby looked up, Mae's eyes were open. As the Indian looked deeply into Ruby's eyes, she grasped the girl by the arms and drew her close to her face.

In a weak, whispery voice, Mae told Ruby how much she loved her. Before she departed to go live with the spirits, she said, she wanted to leave her something—and she began to tell Ruby about the secret gold mine of the Chinook Indians. As a lone flickering candle fought to illuminate the dark room, Mae revealed the location of the mine. When she finished, she sighed deeply and died.

In tears, Ruby informed the family of the death of the old Chinook woman, and preparations were made to bury her on the morrow.

Following the funeral, Ruby went to her room, took out her journal, and wrote down the directions to the Chinook gold mine just as Mae had given them. The next day, she shared this revelation with the rest of the family. Expecting everyone to be excited about the gold, Ruby was disappointed when they only laughed and told her it was nothing more than an old Indian superstition, that no such mine had ever existed. Disheartened, Ruby placed her journal in a bureau drawer, where it remained for several years.

One day, Melvin White, one of Ruby's older brothers who owned and operated a fish cannery near San Francisco, arrived at Tillamook Bay for a visit. When the two were alone, Melvin asked Ruby if she still possessed the information about the secret gold mine. When she replied she did, Melvin told her that he had given the matter considerable thought and was finally convinced the mine was real and that a fortune in gold ore awaited whomever could locate it. Ruby gave Melvin the directions.

Three weeks later, Melvin loaded a packhorse with mining tools and provisions and departed, alone, for the high country of the Coast Range. Convinced he would find the mine, he smilingly told the rest of his family they would all be rich when he returned.

Nothing was heard from Melvin White for nearly ten years. In the summer of 1917, two hunters found his remains in a remote canyon near Round Top Mountain in the Coast Range. In his skull was a single bullet hole, and his death remains a mystery to this day.

Solomon Emerick owned a large farm near Forest Grove, a community about twenty miles west of downtown Portland. Like the Whites of Tillamook Bay, Emerick often employed Indian workers. One summer, the mother of one of his farmhands came to visit. While she rode around the farm with her son one morning, her horse stumbled and fell, throwing the rider roughly to the ground. When the woman was finally carried back to the farmhouse, it was determined she had broken several bones and was bleeding internally. Emerick, after sending a rider to fetch a doctor from Portland, did everything he could to make the woman's last hours comfortable. The doctor said there was nothing he could do.

As the woman lay dying on the farmer's bed, she thanked Emerick for caring for her and, reaching into a pouch strapped to her waist, withdrew three huge gold nuggets and handed them to him. Startled, Emerick asked where the nuggets came from, and the woman replied that they were from the secret gold mine of the Chinook Indians, which was located in the nearby mountains "in a black canyon where a stream empties into a small lake."

A year later, Emerick undertook a search for the gold mine, and though he spent nearly a full month in the mountains of the Coast Range, he found nothing. In spite of his lack of success, Emerick remained convinced of the existence and richness of the gold mine and, on returning to Forest Grove, sold all of his property and belongings and spent the rest of his life searching for the wealth that somehow always eluded him.

One of Emerick's neighbors was a man named Frank Watrous. Watrous was a relatively young man of twenty-five years when Emerick left his farm to search for the Chinook gold. Fascinated with the story of the secret mine, however, Watrous spent most of his adult years collecting information on it and interviewing Indians and others who might possess some insight relative to its location. Every summer, Watrous spent weeks packing into the Coast Range following leads and information he had accumulated over the years.

After more than a decade of searching, Watrous eventually concentrated his efforts on a remote area near the crest of the range. Here, he claimed, he found a dark canyon containing a stream that flowed into a lake! Nearby, Watrous discovered evidence of more than a dozen Indian campsites, and even found where gold had been separated from the quartz matrix. Here and there in the small piles of quartz, Watrous found tiny gold nuggets that had apparently escaped the notice of the Indians.

In an adjacent canyon, Watrous found evidence of an old mine, but the shaft had been filled in. Convinced it was the secret gold mine of the Chinook, he decided to reopen it.

For weeks, Watrous labored to remove large rocks from the mouth of the tunnel. One day as he was struggling with a particularly large rock, he was surprised by three riders who curtly demanded he explain what he was doing. Not wishing to reveal the existence of the mine to the newcomers, Watrous told them he was going to build a rock cabin at this site. One of the riders spurred his horse forward a few steps and told Watrous he was on private property and to get off immediately.

On at least three other occasions, Watrous entered the canyon to continue to try to clear the shaft, and each time he was discovered and evicted. Frustrated but undaunted, Watrous continued to research tales of the secret Chinook mine, but died in an automobile accident before was able to return to the canyon.

Concentrated research into the legend and lore of the secret gold mine of the Chinook Indians has convinced many scholars that it was real. Though apparently well hidden, it likely exists to this day, and the chances are excellent that it has not been entered since the Indians covered the entrance around a hundred years ago. Its presumed location has been identified by several who have studied existing journals and other documents, but this purportedly rich mine is located on private property, whose current owner for many years resisted all recovery attempts.

In 1979, three treasure hunters who surreptitiously entered the canyon containing the mine were discovered and fired upon. One man received a serious wound, and all three were charged with trespassing. At this writing, however, a recovery company is negotiating with the property owner. Perhaps in the near future the secret gold mine of the Chinook will be reopened.

WASHINGTON

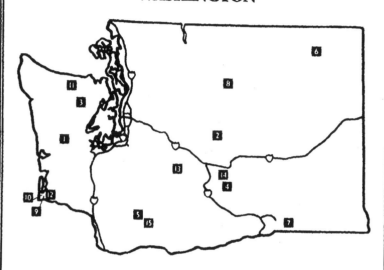

1. Buried Treasure of the Wynoochee River Wildman
2. Scottish Lord's Buried Treasure Chest
3. Skeletons and Gold in the Olympic Mountains
4. Lost "Two Saddles" Gold Cache
5. Lost Mexican Gold in the Cascade Range
6. Gold Lost Four Times!
7. Outlaw Gold Buried Near Fort Walla Walla
8. Indian Mission Gold Cache
9. Gold Cache of the Eccentric Salvor
10. Treasure in the Well
11. Port Discovery Gold
12. Lost Gold Cache of James Scarborough
13. Recent Gold Nugget Discoveries in Kittitas County
14. Columbia River Payroll Gold
15. Lost Skeleton Gold Mine

Buried Treasure of the Wynoochee River Wildman

When John Turnow was a very young boy it was obvious to everyone who saw him that he was different. For one thing, he was huge for his age; at ten years old he was as large as many grown men. For another, he shunned the company of others, even his own family, and spent most of his time alone in the woods.

When Turnow was fifteen years of age, he stood six feet, four inches tall and weighed 250 pounds, all muscle. He seldom stayed with his parents in the crude log home they occupied in Satsop. Instead, he regularly fled into the woods, where he sometimes remained for weeks, foraging for food and sleeping in caves and hollow logs.

By the time he was thirty years old, John Turnow was a permanent resident of the forests and mountains in the Wynoochee River region of Grays Harbor County. The reclusive giant garnered a reputation as a crack shot with a rifle, and he occasionally brought down game with impressive efficiency and marksmanship. Turnow lived contentedly in the wilderness—with wild game, berries, and roots abundant—and rarely entered town. He was soon known as the Wynoochee River Wildman, and his sudden and silent appearances in the deep forests often frightened and unnerved prospectors, loggers, and hunters.

Turnow preferred the solitude of the dense, lonely woods to the stares and jokes of the townsfolk. John Turnow, it was claimed by many, was insane, and one of these days, they promised, he was going to hurt somebody.

In July of 1909, Turnow's father had him committed to an insane asylum where he was, for all intents and purposes, caged like a wild animal. Unable to bear the restraints imposed on him at the asylum, Turnow escaped after only a few weeks and fled once again deep into his beloved and comfortable woods.

Now and then, Turnow was spotted by hunters or loggers, who described him as a "giant, bearded, gorilla-like creature completely at home in the forest, often running like a deer." While Turnow never hurt anyone, woodsmen were generally afraid of him.

In September 1911, Turnow shot and killed a steer grazing in a meadow. As he was cutting the haunches from the animal, a shot rang out from behind. He turned to discover the owner of the steer, along with another man, walking toward him, rifles at their sides.

Almost casually, Turnow raised his own rifle, fired two well-placed shots, and killed both men—one with a bullet in the middle of the forehead, the other shot through the left eye. Shouldering the meat he cut from the steer, Turnow calmly walked away and into the woods.

When the two dead men—who, as it turned out, were brothers—were discovered the following morning, a posse, under the leadership of Deputy Sheriff Colin McKenzie, fanned out into the rain forest in search of Turnow.

Turnow, aware he was being pursued, fled deep into the valley of the Wynoochee River. While lawmen and dogs tracked him, the Wildman easily kept just ahead of the posse and out of sight. During his flight, he passed through several of the small lumber camps found in the area—Aberdeen, Elma, Hoquiam, Jackson, and Montesano.

Somehow, residents of these tiny settlements received word that Turnow had killed two men and was "on the loose" and "on a wild killing rampage up the Wynoochee River Valley." In the camps, men and women armed themselves with rifles and pistols and stayed constantly on the watch for the Wildman.

One night, following a six-inch snowfall, Turnow quietly arrived at the outskirts of the small settlement of Jackson. Moving silently behind and between the wooded frame buildings that made up most of the town, the mountain man spotted the grocery store, a single-story, elongated frame shack located near the center of the little community. When hungry, Turnow had occasionally broken into stores in the small lumber camps found throughout the region. After running from his pursuers for three days without eating, Turnow decided to procure some food. He moved closer to the store.

Turnow found an unlocked window at the rear of the store, quickly opened it, and climbed in. Once inside, he gathered some beans, bacon, matches, and ammunition for his rifle. As he was leaving, he spotted a small metal box on the counter. Opening the container, he found nearly $20,000 in gold coins and bills. Unknown to the wild man, the store also served as a bank for the tiny community, and the money represented the total deposits of Jackson's residents. Well aware of what money could provide, Turnow secured the lid to the box and stuffed it into one of the wide pockets of his tattered coat.

Milton Jackson, the owner of the store and bank, lived next door. In the middle of the night he was awakened by a slight noise coming from the store. Pulling on his boots and grabbing his rifle, Jackson set out to investigate and arrived just in time to see Turnow running into the nearby woods, arms filled with stolen goods.

The following morning, Jackson wasted no time in posting a $1,000 reward for the capture of John Turnow. When word of the reward money got around, the number of men in the woods swelled to more than two hundred, all of them armed. The over-eager trackers began shooting at anything that moved in the forest. One of the searchers, a seventeen-year-old boy, was shot by one of the posse members who mistook him for Turnow.

But they never found the Wildman. Though a few of the more persistent trackers remained in the woods for several days, hopeful of capturing or killing the fugitive and claiming the reward money, the posse formally disbanded and most of the hunters returned to their homes.

During the first week of March 1912, Turnow was spotted near Oxbow, a location on the upper reaches of the Wynoochee River where the stream course swings around in a sharp meander. Here, a prospector named Lighe McKinnon spotted Turnow roasting meat over a campfire. Realizing this was the notorious Wildman of the Wynoochee, McKinnon, afraid of being discovered, simply sat back and observed Turnow. At one point during his meal, according to McKinnon, Turnow pulled the metal box from his coat pocket and removed a great handful of bills and coins. McKinnon said the killer spent nearly an hour stacking the bills and coins in separate piles, counting and recounting them.

After Turnow laid down by the fire and fell asleep, McKinnon quietly crept away and notified Deputy Sheriff McKenzie. McKenzie, preferring not to lead another large group of men into the forest, contacted Game Warden Albert Elmer, and together the two men hiked deep into the remote Oxbow country in search of Turnow. Eventually, they found the campfire, and nearby Elmer discovered three of the gold coins taken from the Jackson store. They found no trace of Turnow.

On March 16, Deputy Sheriff A.L. Fitzgerald was given the responsibility of organizing yet another posse to enter the forest and capture the elusive Turnow. Unfortunately, storekeeper–banker Jackson upped the reward to $2,000, and the woods once again filled with armed and eager men, each believing they would find and kill the Wildman.

Days passed. The hunt continued, but the pursuers gradually dropped out. On April 13, three deputies, searching in an area about a mile upstream from Oxbow, discovered a crudely fashioned shelter made from bark and spruce boughs. As they approached the shelter, a shot rang out from within and one of the deputies collapsed to the ground, a bullet between his eyes. Another shot came from the bark structure, and yet another deputy fell, this one with a bullet though the heart.

The remaining lawman, Giles Quinby, scrambled frantically to reach the shelter of the trunk of a large tree. After nearly ten minutes of trying to regain his composure, Quinby called to Turnow and told him all he wanted was to recover the money he had taken from Jackson's store.

Turnow responded by saying he had buried the money near his campfire back at Oxbow next to a boulder that looked like the fin of a large fish. With that, he rose and fired a shot at Quinby, the bullet splitting bark off the covering tree. Quinby quickly released a volley of shots but could not tell what effect they had on Turnow. For more than an hour it was quiet in the bark shack, but Quinby was too frightened to advance.

Nearly two hours later, Quinby was joined by several other posse members, and together the men, rifles at the ready, crept toward the shelter.

Behind the lean-to, the large, ape-like form of John Turnow lay in death, killed from the effect of several of Quinby's bullets striking him in the head and chest.

Several days later, Deputy Quinby hiked to Turnow's old campsite near Oxbow, determined to find the $20,000 taken from the Jackson store. After several minutes of searching, he found the boulder that resembled a fish's fin, and proceeded to make several excavations at its base. He found nothing.

The few who knew John Turnow believed the wild man was telling the truth when he said the money had been buried near the Oxbow campsite. Turnow may have been strange, even retarded, they all testified, but he was incapable of telling a lie. If he claimed he buried the money near the fin-shaped boulder at Oxbow, they all said, then it was a safe bet the loot was there.

The $20,000 hidden by John Turnow, the Wildman of the Wynoochee, would be worth much more today, especially the gold coins. Metal detectors were by and large unavailable when Deputy Quinby searched for the loot back in 1912, but if he had owned one he likely would have had a better chance of locating the loot. Today, a hardy outdoorsman, willing to hike the rugged up-country terrain of the Wynoochee River, and in possession of a good metal detector, might get lucky and find a small fortune somewhere near a boulder that looks like the fin of a fish located in the Oxbow country of the Wynoochee River.

Scottish Lord's Buried Treasure Chest

Sometime early in the summer of 1889, Thomas Douglas, a Scottish nobleman and son of the Earl and Countess of Angus, arrived on America's shores determined to carve out a new life for himself in the growing nation, a nation that held promise for many a European immigrant. Among Douglas's personal belongings was a large, heavy wooden chest, reinforced with copper cornering and bound with stout leather straps. Douglas supervised the unloading of his effects, and as he, draped in an elegant, expensive cape and top hat, led the way down the gangplank to the loading dock, several stewards followed behind carrying trunks, bags of clothing, and other items. Though the heavy wooden chest was no larger than a peach crate, it took two strong men to transport it. Unknown to the pair of laborers, the chest was filled to the top with gold coins, the Douglas family fortune.

Many have speculated on why Thomas Douglas migrated to America, leaving a life of ease and comfort in Scotland. Relatives claimed that it was because the adventurous Scotsman sought new and exciting opportunities in the United States. It was often whispered around the inns and taverns of Douglas's home village of Perth, however, that the charming heir had fled the country after having been surprised in a compromising position with the wife of a close friend.

For three years, Douglas wandered throughout New York, Pennsylvania, and along the Middle Atlantic Coast, seeking business ventures into which he might invest a portion of his fortune. He found little that appealed to him and instead began to listen intently to the stories of lumbering, ranching, and mining opportunities awaiting the energetic and aspiring investor far across the country in the Pacific Northwest. Intrigued by the possibilities of profit and adventure he believed to lie in the Northwest, Douglas packed his bags and struck out for Washington and the Cascade Range.

Eventually, Douglas settled into the tiny community of Blewett in Chelan County, north-central Washington, where he invested in several mining claims, none of which provided the excitement and profit for which the Scotsman longed.

Always a heavy drinker, Douglas continued to pursue this habit after moving to Blewett, and his cabin was often the scene of two- and three-day-long drinking bouts and poker games. It was said that Douglas made more money from playing poker than he did from his business interests.

One cold, snowy December evening in 1905, Douglas invited several friends over to his cabin for a high-stakes poker game. Hours later, most of the card players, one by one, dropped out, unable to cover the high and sometimes exorbitant bets. After several more hours passed, the game continued with only Douglas and two others, the rest having made their way home through the snow and winds.

After a run of bad luck, Douglas found himself critically short of money. As the wagering grew heavier, the Scotsman called for a brief halt in the game and, as his two friends watched, he dragged a heavy wooden chest from a nearby closet over to the table and opened it. Much to the astonishment of his two guests, it was filled with gold and silver coins! From the chest, Douglas pulled out a handful of money, enough to allow him to continue playing.

Several days later, word of Douglas's incredible fortune spread throughout Blewett. Concerned that he might be robbed, Douglas secured the leather straps on the trunk and, in the dark of night, dragged it out into the yard to bury it. As the snow fell and the wind whipped cold air up his flapping pantlegs, Douglas laboriously excavated a hole in the nearly frozen ground.

About sixty yards from Douglas's cabin lived Hazel Winesapp, a widow with three children who eked out a living by taking in wash from the Blewitt residents. That same night, while nursing a sick child, she caught a glimpse through her window of her neighbor Douglas out in his yard. In spite of the somewhat obscuring haze of falling snow, Hazel Winesapp could barely see Douglas's form in the weak glow of his lantern. Presently, the widow watched the Scotsman lower something heavy into the hole and cover it up. Believing her neighbor was only burying some garbage, Hazel Winesapp went on ministering to her ailing daughter.

Two months later two young brothers, William and Frederick Burmeister, were hunting rabbits near the Douglas cabin. As they trudged through the deep snow in the middle of the afternoon, they noticed a lantern was burning inside the dwelling, even though it was midday and the sun was shining brightly. The brothers peeked in one of the windows and saw Douglas lying on his bed. He appeared to be dead.

The Burmeister brothers ran as quickly as they could for help. The first person they encountered was the postmaster, Henry Reisberg. Reisberg went at once to the cabin and found Douglas alive but paralyzed, probably from a stroke. The Scotsman was taken immediately to Reisberg's home where the postmaster's wife could care for him. In spite of Mrs. Reisberg's efforts, Douglas passed away quietly in his sleep two days later.

Under the supervision of postmaster Reisberg, a contingent of men from Blewett searched the Douglas cabin for the fortune in gold and silver coins they knew the Scottish nobleman possessed. Though they pulled up floorboards and removed planks from the wall, they found nothing of any value.

In May 1908, the widow Hazel Winesapp, during a conversation with a Blewett storekeeper, Roland Henze, mentioned observing the late Thomas Douglas bury something in his yard not far from the cabin. Because it had been nearly three years, Winesapp was not certain exactly where in the yard the excavation took place.

Widow Winesapp's revelation caused a stampede of treasure seekers to descend on the old Douglas property. Dozens of holes were excavated but, again, nothing was found.

The treasure of Scotsman Thomas Douglas, son of the Earl and Countess of Angus, has never been recovered. Today, it is likely worth well over a million dollars.

Skeletons and Gold in the Olympic Mountains

During the first week of October in 1900, a time of dropping temperatures, low fog, and persistent rain, James Hogg, a professional hunter, packed into a remote portion of the Olympic Mountains in search of game. What he eventually discovered was a ridge top covered with skeletons and gold nuggets, gold so plentiful that it almost covered the ground over a wide area.

Hogg was a contract hunter for several restaurants and stores doing business in communities along the Hood Canal, Dabob Bay, and the Strait of Juan de Fuca. As was his custom, Hogg traveled deep into the mountain range several times each year leading a team of packhorses, durable mountain-bred animals he hoped to load with freshly killed game, which he would carry back and market to his customers.

On this particular hunting trip, Hogg followed an old, narrow, little-used trail that wound around the southwestern portion of The Brothers Peak, a 6,866-foot prominence that dominates this section of the Olympics.

Around midafternoon of the third day of his expedition, Hogg encountered abundant signs of elk and deer and, as he still had about three hours of daylight remaining, quickly set up camp and went in search of game. About thirty minutes later, Hogg spotted a twelve-point buck browsing among some low-growing brush on the opposite side of the meadow from where he crouched. The deer, immediately alert to the hunter's presence, bounded away. As it fled, Hogg raised his rifle and fired quickly, wounding the animal. Cursing his haste and careless aim, he set out to track the animal.

Hogg followed droplets of blood through the forest for nearly an hour, but the deer managed to stay far ahead of the pursuer and out of sight. Hogg traveled generally northward and crossed two low ridges during his pursuit; once, when he paused to look around, he realized he was in a part of the Olympic Range he had never before seen. As the light of the day grew dimmer, James Hogg also realized he was lost. When it was well into dusk, the hunter was hurrying back through the thick forest in what he thought was the general direction of his campsite.

Unable to relocate the route along which he has just traveled, Hogg soon found himself hopelessly confused in the moonless woods, a forest darker and more foreboding than anything he had ever experienced in his entire life as an outdoorsman. Afraid to proceed in the stygian darkness, he climbed into the lower branches of a tree and spent a cold night perched on a thick limb about fifteen feet above the ground. All night long, the nervous Hogg listened to the growling of foraging bears and the screams of mountain lions.

With dawn, Hogg climbed down from the tree and continued hiking in the direction in which he thought his camp was located. Approaching a low ridge, Hogg was certain it was one he had crossed the previous evening, and he made his way to the top. As he crested the ridge, he saw that the top held only thinly scattered, stunted trees, precariously surviving on the thin soil that remained on what was for the most part a bare rock outcrop. But Hogg saw something else, something that took his breath away and raised the hairs along his forearm and the back of his neck, something he never forgot for the rest of his life.

Scattered across a portion of the ridge, in a space spanning approximately ten square yards, were the skeletal remains of at least a half-dozen men. On some of the skeletons, items such as leather belts, boots, and suspenders remained, though their dried and cracked appearance suggested they had lain exposed for many years. Weathered saddlebags lay nearby, as did rusted picks and shovels.

As Hogg walked among the grisly array of human remains, his eye caught the glint of sparkling stones, small brightly colored nuggets densely scattered among the bones. After retrieving one of the larger stones, one about the size of a pumpkin seed, Hogg was astonished to discover it was almost pure gold! He quickly examined several others and found they, too, were gold. He stuffed nearly three pounds of the rich nuggets into his coat pockets.

As Hogg studied the scene before him, he deduced that the skeletons represented a party of miners that had likely been surprised and killed, perhaps by Indians. The Indians who had inhabited this area, as Hogg knew, cared little for the glittering metal, a fact that accounted for the gold that was left lying on the ground.

Hogg decided to find his camp as quickly as possible, return to his home at Brinnon on Dabob Bay, and make arrangements for an expedition back to this gold nugget-covered ridge. As he cautiously made his way down the steep west side of the ridge, Hogg tripped over some vines and tumbled and rolled to the bank of the narrow stream below. When he finally stood up and dusted himself off, he discovered he had lost his rifle and badly sprained his ankle. Afraid of being unarmed in an unfamiliar wilderness, Hogg panicked and, with a pronounced and painful limp, fled deep into the forest.

Days later, an exhausted and emaciated Hogg arrived at a farmhouse located near the present-day town of Queets on the Pacific Ocean side of the Olympic Peninsula. There, he was taken in and cared for until he was able to travel. Hogg told his hosts of his frightening flight through the unfamiliar forest, surviving on berries and frogs. It was said that Hogg's hair, normally a dark brown, had turned completely white as a result of his ordeal.

During the second week of his stay at the farmhouse, Hogg showed his new friends his pocketsful of gold nuggets and told them of his amazing find. Later, Hogg sold the gold for a total of $800.

When the story of the gold discovery became known throughout the Olympic Peninsula, many fortune hunters, eager to find the location, attempted to get Hogg to lead them. In spite of offers of several thousand dollars from several different groups of investors, Hogg flatly refused, stating he never wanted to enter the forest again. Hogg eventually moved to California where he lived out his life working in a mercantile.

Though many have searched through dozens of history books and interviewed several score of old-timers living on the Olympic Peninsula, no one has ever encountered an explanation for the existence of the skeletons and the gold on the mysterious ridge. A corresponding mystery has to do with the gold itself: during recorded history, there has never been any kind of gold mining in this part of the Olympic Peninsula. What was the source of the gold found among the skeletal remains on the top of that mysterious ridge? Was it mined nearby? Was it only being transported through the area? Where had they come from? Where were they bound? Who were these men, dead for at least twenty years when discovered by James Hogg?

As far as anyone knows, the human remains and the fortune in scattered gold nuggets found by the lost hunter still lies atop the lost rock outcrop somewhere near The Brothers Peak in the eastern Olympic Mountains.

Lost "Two Saddles" Gold Cache

In 1871, John Welch, a Portland businessman, sold his home, store, and small tract of land, loaded his wife and daughter into a sturdy covered wagon drawn by two oxen, and departed for the wilds of British Columbia to dig for gold.

For years, Welch had listened to miners' tales of striking it rich in the streams and exposed granite rocks deep in the British Columbian Rockies. By contrast, the life of a hardware and grocery merchant offered little excitement: the days were long, the work was tedious, and stimulating challenges rarely surfaced. Unable to contain his desire to journey to Canada to try his luck in the goldfields any longer, Welch confessed his dreams to his family and, with their support and company, departed to find his fortune.

After arriving in the British Columbian Rockies three months later, the Welch family lived out of the back of the wagon for six months. While the women tended camp, John Welch explored the many canyons, panned the streams, searched the rock mountainsides for signs of color, and visited with experienced prospectors and miners, listening to their tales and learning much from their gold-hunting adventures.

The months wore on, then years, and Welch had little or no luck finding gold. Close to the point of total discouragement, with his savings nearly exhausted Welch was about to decide to pack up and return to Portland when he finally found the gold for which he had searched so long and hard. In a remote canyon containing a narrow, shallow, clear-water stream, Welch gazed at several gleaming gold nuggets reflecting in his oft-used pan. Working his way up and down the tiny stream, Welch found gold everywhere he dipped his pan. His excitement was so great, he panned throughout the day and on into the night, not pausing for food or rest for nearly thirty hours. Two days later, the exhausted Welch stumbled into his camp, and as his relieved wife and daughter watched, he dumped several ounces of nuggets of pure gold onto a calico cloth he spread out near the campfire.

Within two days, the Welch family had moved their camp to the mouth of the canyon containing the gold-filled stream, and soon man, woman, and child were all panning for the abundant gold that lay in the shallow water. It was 1876, and after six months of hard, consistent work, the Welches had accumulated about $100,000 worth of gold. Now wealthy beyond his wildest imaginings, Welch began to miss Portland, and he talked often about returning. Furthermore, he was anxious to enroll his daughter in a proper school. After discussing the matter for several days, the Welches finally packed up, loaded their gold nuggets into several canvas mineral sacks, and headed back to Oregon.

Days later, they arrived at the Columbia River at a point in what is now Grant County. As they traveled along the trail paralleling the great stream searching for a suitable crossing, they eventually encountered the tiny settlement of Trinidad. Here the Welches were warned about rampaging Indians in the area. During the past month, Welch was told, Indians had attacked and killed several miners and all the members of a small wagon train.

Welch, not wanting to remain in Trinidad any longer, decided to continue. He told several Trinidad townsfolk he intended to bury his gold somewhere along the river and return with an escort of soldiers from one of the nearby forts to retrieve it. The citizens thought Welch foolish to subject his family to the dangers of the trail, but he was adamant and lashed his oxen toward Portland.

That evening, Welch stopped to make camp where a stream flowed into the Columbia River. The stream exited out of a canyon, wide at the mouth but narrowing dramatically toward the upstream end.

Loading his gold onto two of the horses he acquired in Canada, Welch rode into the canyon, selected a suitable site, and buried his fortune in nuggets. Following this, he walked about thirty yards downslope and proceeded to excavate a wider, deeper hole. Into this he placed the two packsaddles carried by the horses, along with several other items, including his wife's comb and brush, a small wooden box containing important papers, and several hair ribbons of different colors. After refilling the hole with dirt, Welch built a cairn of rocks on top of it, carefully piling the stones until they reached about four feet high.

The next morning found the Welch family once again on the trail in search of a crossing. They had ridden no more than a mile from the camp they had just abandoned when they were set upon by Indians. While several angry-looking braves surrounded the family, three others pulled the Welches from the wagon and climbed into it in search of goods. After taking only several items of clothing and Welch's hat, they departed, leaving the travelers frightened but unharmed.

Relieved at being spared their lives, the Welch family traveled to Fort Vancouver, the closest military outpost, and reported the incident. When he requested an escort so he could return to the area to retrieve his gold, Welch was denied. The post commander informed him he had no men to spare. Welch had no choice but to proceed to Portland and attempt a return when the threat of hostile Indians had been removed from the region.

Somehow Welch needed to provide a living for himself and his family. He obtained a job as a clerk in the same store he had once owned and settled into a two-room cabin just outside of town. Eventually, Welch acquired some land and purchased some livestock; he threw himself into the businesses of raising cattle and cutting timber for the growing city of Portland. Though his thoughts never strayed far from the buried cache of gold nuggets miles away near the Columbia River, he remained quite busy with his new business ventures.

Finally, in 1904, John Welch returned to Trinidad to find his gold and carry it back to Portland. On arriving in the area, however, he found himself quite unprepared for the changes he encountered. The town of Trinidad had grown, new roads had been cut throughout the region, and the hills were scraped bare of timber as a result of intensive logging. Erosion of the now-denuded mountain slopes had created deep gullies, and vast portions of some hillsides had been almost completely eroded away. Welch recognized little about the region.

After an unsuccessful search along the Columbia River for the canyon in which he had buried his gold, Welch returned to town, told his story to two men he believed he could trust, and hired them as guides to help him find his cache. Though the trio entered and explored several canyons that intersected the mighty Columbia, none contained the rock cairn constructed by Welch over the two saddles. Discouraged, Welch gave up the search and returned to Portland, where he tried his best to recall the riverside landscape of twenty-eight years earlier. From memory, he drew a crude map showing the canyon in which he had buried the gold and the approximate location of the rock cairn. He gave the map to his daughter, Anna, and told her to try to find the fortune someday. Three months later, John Welch died in his sleep.

Anna Welch, who was by this time married to William Tuttle, conducted at least six searches for the lost gold, all of them ending in failure. She firmly believed her late father's map was accurate, but she confessed to having difficulty following the directions. Anna Tuttle died in 1929 and her map has never been found.

In 1931, two trappers—H.B. Welby and Wapiti Ted Williams—snared a bobcat in a small canyon near the Columbia River. The snare was anchored to a large pile of rocks found earlier by the two men. When they returned to check their trap, they discovered the bobcat had attempted to dig a small shelter under the rocks. Looking closely into the hole excavated by the animal, Welby spotted part of a saddle. After pulling down the rock cairn and enlarging the hole, the two trappers found another saddle, a wooden box containing some legal papers, and some colored ribbon—all of the items buried by Welch fifty-five years earlier!

When word of the discovery spread throughout the area, several residents knowledgeable about the lost gold cache of John Welch went to the canyon to search for it. Hundreds of holes were dug, but nothing was ever found. Experts who have carefully researched the Welch story claim that the search for the gold and the subsequent excavations took place too close to the location where the saddles were discovered. The gold cache, they maintain, was at least thirty yards away and uphill.

Years later, Wanapum Dam was constructed a short distance downstream near the small town of Beverly. It is believed by some that the canyon in which John Welch cached his fortune in gold nuggets has been inundated by the water behind the dam.

As this is being written, two men who live in Seattle have conducted extensive research on the John Welch story and are convinced they know the location of the cache are preparing to attempt an underwater search. The gold, which would be worth in excess of $2,000,000 dollars today, is believed to be located in calm shallow water easily accessible to searchers with scuba gear.

Lost Mexican Gold in the Cascade Range

Somewhere near the headwaters of the Lewis River in a relatively remote section of the Cascade Range between Mount St. Helens and Mount Adams lies a rich deposit of gold. The evidence for the existence of this ore is abundant, but the location of the rich lode has eluded searchers for over a century. It may be, perhaps, the most fascinating lost mine tale in the entire state of Washington, and the search for what likely amounts to millions of dollars worth of gold continues today.

This tale has its beginnings in 1881. During the early autumn of that year, an elderly Mexican was often observed by hunters and trappers coming out of the Cascade Range, following the route of the southwestern-bound Lewis River. Somewhere just west of Steamboat Rock Mountain, the Mexican, leading three heavily laden pack mules, turned southeastward and followed the low passes through the Pacific Crest and into the Klickitat Valley. After reaching the Klickitat River, he stopped at the small settlements along its banks, purchased supplies, and visited with the townsfolk. The Mexican, who spoke passable English, always paid for his purchases with gold, which he withdrew from one of the heavy packs tied to the horses. A congenial sort, he delighted in visiting with the settlers in the area and often bought candy treats for the youngsters.

Eventually, after a long journey, the Mexican arrived at The Dalles on the banks of the Columbia River, where he stopped at the French and Company Bank, carried several heavy saddlebags inside, and dumped a fortune in gold ore onto the director's desk. With the help of three assistants, the gold was weighed, valued, and converted into cash, which was then deposited into the Mexican's account.

An assayer who was given the responsibility of evaluating the Mexican's gold stated it was the purest he had seen in his lifetime and that it had apparently been excavated from a quartz vein that evidently intruded into Cascade Range granite.

On three other occasions during the next two years, the Mexican made similar deposits, each time leading three pack mules bearing gold from his diggings into town. It was estimated that the Mexican eventually deposited a total of about $1 million—the earnings from his fabulous secret gold mine.

As was generally the case when a significant gold discovery became known, curious men attempted to follow the Mexican back to his mine. The Mexican, aware he was being watched, successfully eluded and confused his trackers by pulling the shoes from the hooves of his horse and mules and nailing them on backwards. The trackers always lost their quarry somewhere after crossing the White Salmon River southwest of Mount Adams. Because hunters and trappers had often seen the Mexican either riding up or coming down the trail that paralleled the Lewis River, they presumed his secret mine lay near the headwaters of that stream.

In 1885, the Mexican, as was his custom, arrived at The Dalles, made a huge deposit, and remained in town for a few days. Then he departed and rode away toward the northwest, leading his mules. It was the last time he was ever seen.

During the next two years, residents of the area noticed that local Indians were using gold to pay for goods they purchased in town. When asked how they came into possession of the gold, most remained mute to the question, but several pointed back into the mountains in the general direction of the headwaters of the Lewis River. It was rumored for months that the Indians had attacked and killed the Mexican coming out of the mountains and took his gold, but this was never proven. Others were convinced the Indians knew the location of the Mexican's secret mine and excavated gold from it from time to time.

About two years later, a party of trappers discovered the skeletal remains of a man and three mules. Scattered about the gruesome collection of bones were the rotted remains of packsaddles, saddlebags, bits and harnesses, and camping gear. It was assumed these were the remains of the Mexican and his stock.

In 1889, a second Mexican, a much younger one, arrived in the region and settled onto a small tract of land near Bickelton in Klickitat County. Though not unfriendly, the newcomer was somewhat reclusive, often disappearing for weeks at a time into the Cascade Range between Mount St. Helens and Mount Adams. The Mexican identified himself as Juan Rabado (some accounts refer to him, strangely enough, as Pierre, and in others his surname is sometimes given as Rablado, sometimes as Rablando). One day Rabado arrived in Bickelton with two small canvas pouches containing gold nuggets, which he used to pay for some goods. During subsequent conversation with the storekeeper, Rabado claimed he dug the gold from a location on the other side of Mount Adams, and that he had been given a map of the location by his father, who mined the gold several years earlier.

After purchasing several months' worth of food and supplies, Rabado rode into the Cascade Range leading three pack animals. Like the older Mexican, Rabado was never seen again.

Amos White, a cattle rancher who owned a large spread in the White Salmon River Valley, had worked in the

California gold mines as a youth and never quite lost his lust for the mineral. White was aware of the trips Rabado made from the mountains into town and of the great amounts of gold he carried. White's curiosity was aroused and he wondered often and aloud about where the gold had come from. White attempted to follow the young man on at least two occasions but was unsuccessful.

One day in 1892, a Yakima Indian arrived at White's ranch asking for a meal. White fed the Indian some stew out by the pens, and visited with him while he ate. While talking with the Yakima, White noticed he was carrying a canvas mineral sack that appeared to be very heavy. After asking what it contained, the Indian opened it and showed the rancher: it was nearly filled with gold nuggets, hundreds of them! When asked where they came from, the Indian explained to White that they were dug from a mine near the headwaters of the Lewis River.

White asked the Indian if he would lead him to the mine, but the Yakima refused, saying it meant death at the hands of tribal members to show a white man such things. White promised to pay the Indian $1,000 a year for the rest of his life, telling him he could move to town and never have to work again. The Yakima eventually agreed to the proposition, and White made plans to leave for the Lewis River the next morning.

While eating dinner at a campsite on the second evening of their journey, White and the Yakima were surprised by the sudden appearance of about a dozen Indians, all armed, their bodies and faces painted crimson and white. When White asked what they wanted, they stated gruffly they only wished to speak to the Yakima. Fearfully, White's guide walked a few yards out into the woods and spoke with the visitors in low tones.

Several minutes later, the Yakima returned to camp and began to pack his belongings. When White asked what was going on, the Indian told him that if the two of them were to proceed any further toward the site of the gold mine, they would both be killed. The Indian told White that he was returning immediately to the White Salmon River Valley.

After the Yakima departed, White remained in camp. The following day, he decided to continue on toward the location where he believed the mine to be. The rancher was confident he had gleaned enough directional information from the Indian to locate the gold.

Two weeks later, rancher White arrived at a small settlement that today is called Trout Lake. Exhausted, dirty, unshaven, and wearing tattered clothes, White claimed he had found the secret mine, had been attacked by Indians, and was forced to fight his way out of the area. To the astonishment of onlookers, he emptied his pockets of about $3,000 worth of nuggets of nearly pure gold he said he had dug from the mine.

Three months passed, and White, determined to return to the mine, organized an expedition that consisted of himself and four neighboring ranchers. In the summer of 1893, White led the party into the Lewis River Valley, but after several days of wandering aimlessly around the region, he confessed to being lost and confused about directions, landmarks, and distance. The disappointed group remained in the range for several days and finally returned to their homes near the White Salmon River. Until his death several years later, White maintained the existence of the lost mine, claiming it was located only about twenty miles north-northwest of Trout Lake. If true, this would place it near the headwaters of the Lewis River, as many had previously assumed.

Sometime during the late 1920s, a rodeo was held at the town of Yakima. The event was well-attended by whites and Indians alike, and hundreds were gathered in the parade ground outside the arena where food and drink were being served. One Indian became quite drunk and loud and began showing around a leather pouch filled with gold nuggets. Several who saw the gold claimed it was of excellent quality and wondered how the Indian obtained it. Eventually, the Indian, after being treated to several more drinks by curious onlookers, admitted he had found the secret mine of the Mexican and that the gold he carried in his pouch was nothing compared to the riches that could be dug from the shaft located in the Cascade Range. As several Yakima Indians looked on, two white men coaxed the reveler to lead them to the mine in the morning. The Indian agreed. The men shook hands and made plans to leave at sunrise. As the white men walked away in one direction and the Indian in another, the small group of Yakimas that had observed the agreement silently followed their drunken comrade into the night.

The next day, as the early morning sun sparkled off the rippling surface of the Yakima River, the eager treasure hunters searched the area for their Indian guide. Finally, they found him under a nearby wagon; his throat had been cut.

Did the slain Indian truly know the location of the Lost Mexican Mine? It is likely he did; otherwise he probably would not have been slain by his fellow tribesmen.

A careful study of this mysterious lost mine suggests to the researcher that it did, in fact, exist. Mineralogical studies of this region indicate the presence of gold, and some mining has taken place. If the Lost Mexican Mine is a reality, as it most assuredly is, it could be one of the richest lost lodes in the state of Washington, perhaps even North America.

Gold Lost Four Times!

For the most part, simply finding gold is a difficult enough task. For some people, holding on to the gold they find often proves to be just as difficult. In northwestern Washington, a fortune in gold currently lies hidden beneath the grassy greens of a golf course, where it was lost for a fourth time!

In the late 1890s, Northport, Washington, located just a couple of miles south of the Canadian border, was once the site of the LeRoy Smelter, a large operation that processed most of the ore that was dug from the Silver Star and LeRoy Mines near Rossland, British Columbia, approximately ten miles to the north. Several times each week, wagonloads of ore-bearing rock were hauled to the smelter where it was crushed, the mineral removed, and the ore processed into ingots. Each year for as long as it remained in operation, the LeRoy Smelter processed millions of dollars' worth of gold.

Then, as now, a problem many smelter owners had to contend with related to glomming the ore. A glommer was a worker who pocketed small amounts of the ore each day and walked off the premises with it. Over time, an effective glommer could make tens of thousands of dollars in this manner. Brokers from clandestine operations sometimes hung around smelters, encouraging the workers to finger a few ounces of ore each week. When the glommer had a sufficient amount of gold or silver, he would then sell it to the broker. A highly skilled glommer could get rich. Some smelting operations claimed they would lose as much as a million dollars' worth of gold a year from ongoing glomming operations.

Glomming was a common practice in those days, and the LeRoy Smelter caught and prosecuted several men caught in the act of stealing the gold.

In the town of Newport, a group of four men decided to go into the glomming business. Each had a history of moving from job to job, not staying long at any of them. Over drinks one evening in a Northport tavern, the four decided stealing gold from the smelter was an easier way of making a living than trying to hold down a job. Two of the men hired on at the smelter and started glomming gold ore on a regular basis. Once a sufficient amount of the gold had accumulated, the other two carried it to Portland or San Francisco, where they converted it to cash. The gang operated very effectively for several weeks, so much so that they decided to try to increase the amount of gold they were removing from the smelter premises. It proved to be a mistake.

Determined to become as rich as possible in the shortest amount of time, the gang members secreted ore from the smelter at a greater rate, gradually accumulating it in several canvas ore sacks for easy transportation to California. In a relatively short time, they had removed approximately $30,000 to $50,000 worth of gold from the property and packed it into bags.

Unknown to the two workers who were stealing the ore, some fellow employees became aware of their crooked activities and reported the thefts to the smelter manager. As the two men worked at their assigned jobs at the smelter the following day, they noticed that several men in coats and ties were observing their every move. Suspecting they had been tipped off about the glomming, the men nervously went about their tasks. That evening when the plant shut down, they hurried to their comrades to report the suspicious behavior of the plant officials.

Fearing that their glomming enterprise had been uncovered, the four men hastily loaded the ore-filled bags—ten in all—and tied them to two spare horses. Just after sundown, they rode out of Newport, leading the gold-laden packhorses. Southward they traveled toward the city of Miles at the junction of the Columbia and Spokane Rivers where they hoped to board a boat and travel to Portland. At Portland, they intended to convert the gold to cash and flee to California.

Unknown to the four thieves, a small posse was following their tracks. At dawn, as the glommers were preparing breakfast, the posse, about two miles away, was riding toward their camp. As the outlaws put out their fire and loaded their horses, one of them spotted the oncoming posse through the trees. In seconds, the glommers were mounted and lashing their horses down the trail toward the south.

Around midafternoon, the glommers found themselves only a short distance from the town of Colville. About a mile behind them, the posse maintained pursuit. Fearing the packhorses were tiring of the heavy load of gold, and afraid they would be caught with the stolen goods, the men decided to hide it. This may have been their second major mistake.

At a point on the Columbia River called China Bend, one of the gang members spotted a culvert across which spanned a railroad bridge. Hurrying to the culvert, they quickly untied the ore packs from the horses and buried them in a hastily dug shallow hole. Following this, they mounted up and rode into Colville just ahead of the posse.

As the glommers were overtaken and apprehended by the posse and their belongings searched, another group of men carrying a wagonload of whiskey smuggled from Canada chanced to stop at the China Bend railroad culvert to set up camp for the night. While one of the smugglers gathered wood for a cookfire, the others tended to the horses. After unsaddling one of the tired animals, a smuggler spotted a fresh excavation. Curious, he dug into it and discovered the ten sacks filled with gold ore!

The next morning the whiskey smugglers, with their wagon weighted down with a heavy load of gold as well as whiskey, continued on their way into Colville. At the very moment the smugglers rode toward town, the glommers were confessing their misdeeds to the posse and agreeing to lead the lawmen back to the culvert and show them where the gold was buried.

With the town of Colville just in sight, the smugglers noticed a group of men riding toward them in the distance. Suspecting the oncoming riders had knowledge of the gold they had found, the smugglers steered the wagon over to a nearby brick plant and hastily buried the sacks of ore in the yard. Trying to make it appear as though they had merely stopped to rest their horses, the smugglers waited for the party of riders to pass and continue northward. After arriving at Colville about thirty minutes later, the smugglers decided to rest there for a few days before returning to the brickyard to dig up the gold and continue on their way.

As the smugglers were setting up a crude camp on the outskirts of Colville, the glommers, escorted by the posse, arrived at the railroad culvert near China Bend. To the astonishment of all, the gold-filled sacks had clearly been dug up and carried away. Mystified, the party returned to Colville.

Later that same day, the party of men the smugglers had passed earlier returned. The smugglers overheard snippets of conversation among them, just enough to learn that the riders were lawmen in search of the gold they had buried just that afternoon.

Too frightened to remain in town or return to the brickyard to retrieve the gold, the smugglers slipped away to their horses and wagon and rode south out of town, never to return.

For approximately thirty years, the gold remained buried and undisturbed in the hole where it was placed by the whiskey smugglers. The brick plant eventually went out of business, and the property was purchased by Stevens County for use as a poor farm, an eighty-acre plot of land wherein needy people were housed and provided opportunities for employment by farming the fields.

One afternoon, one of the county employees responsible for the maintenance of one of the agricultural fields was inspecting some newly planted rows when he spotted something sticking out of the dirt in one of the furrows. Curious, he dug into the ground and removed five partially rotted canvas sacks. Opening each one, he found what he believed were rock samples. It didn't occur to him that it was gold, but nevertheless he realized it must be something important; otherwise it would not have been buried.

The employee apparently did not notice the remaining five ore-filled sacks in the hole, and after filling it in, he lugged his discovery over to one of the old abandoned brick-plant buildings and hid the sacks under some rubble inside.

The county employee, whose name was Lester, was known to have a drinking habit, and one evening several days after finding the canvas sacks, he talked freely about his discovery to his companions in a Colville tavern. One of the men listened intently to Lester's tale of discovering the canvas bags and recognized the story for what it was. The drinking companion was familiar with the old tale of buried gold often related by area old-timers—gold, according to the legend, hidden somewhere in the brickyard by whiskey smugglers years earlier.

Late that night, after everyone left the bar and went home, the drinking companion walked over to the brick plant, entered the abandoned building, and removed the five sacks of gold. When Lester returned to the site the next day, he was troubled at not finding the sacks where he had hidden them. Stricken with guilt, he immediately revealed the discovery to his superior and confessed to hiding the sacks.

Meanwhile, the man who retrieved the gold from the abandoned building attempted to transport it across the Canadian border, where he hoped to sell it. At the crossing, however, the gold was discovered and seized by customs agents. What eventually became of the five sacks of gold is not known.

A few years later, a retired miner by the name of Ivan Knapp announced the discovery of five bags of gold on the grounds of the old poor farm, obviously the five sacks unnoticed by Lester. Knapp, who estimated the value of the gold at around $20,000, was not prepared for the response to his discovery. Anticipating some publicity in the newspaper, he was surprised when taxpayers clamored for him to turn the gold over to the county since it was found on county property. The combination of the negative publicity, a police investigation, and a visit by a representative from the Internal Revenue Service caused Knapp to regret his announcement. Panicked, he carried the gold-filled sacks to another part of the old brickyard and buried them in five separate holes. The next day he told newspaper reporters that his discovery was actually a hoax, and he denied possession of any gold at all.

For weeks, Knapp was closely watched by townsfolk, law enforcement officials, and a tax collector, all of whom believed he did, in fact, possess the gold and that he would eventually reveal its location. Tiring of being shadowed, Knapp left Colville and moved in with a relative in California. Two years later, the old miner died without ever returning to Colville to retrieve the gold or leaving directions as to where it was buried.

Several researchers intimate with this tale are convinced that the old poor farm location where Knapp buried the ore sacks is part of a parcel of land that is now a golf course. Some treasure hunters—who have followed the strange trail of the gold that has been lost four times to the golf greens—have been chased from the area for digging into the grassy, landscaped course. A party of treasure hunters who sought permission to dig for the gold during the 1950s was denied. Eventually, many of those who were familiar with the tale of hidden gold in the area of the golf course have passed away, and today only a few people around Colville remember the tale at all.

If Knapp's estimate of the value of the gold he claimed he found was $20,000, a 1930s value, then it would be worth several times that amount today.

Outlaw Gold Buried Near Fort Walla Walla

Nate Briley and Jed Kincaid, two out-of-work drifters in their mid-twenties, spent many long, hungry days traveling from the mining fields of Nevada to the mountain ranges in eastern Oregon and Washington in search of work. Having exhausted their finances and energies on some unproductive Nevada silver mines, they decided to give up their dreams of wealth, abandon their idealistic quest, and get day jobs. Unfortunately for Briley and Kincaid, other out-of-work miners and newcomers flocking into this region had filled what few available jobs existed in the region, and the two men often found themselves living in the woods in a shabby canvas tent and hunting game for food.

One sunny afternoon the two friends found themselves sitting in the shade of the loading dock of the Rawhide Railroad in Walla Walla. Only moments earlier, Briley and Kincaid had sought work from the owner, Dorsey Baker, but were turned down. Pondering their next move, the young men smoked hand-rolled cigarettes as they watched several workers busily loading goods from a guarded shed into one of the railroad cars.

While eavesdropping on a nearby conversation, Briley and Kincaid learned the railroad company was shipping a small chest filled with several gold ingots to the town of

Wallula on the Columbia River, about thirty miles to the west, where it would be transferred to a steamer. Baker's Rawhide Railroad, which ran between the two towns, seldom transported items of such value; most of their cargo normally consisted of agricultural products harvested from the nearby fields. The rich gold shipment generated an air of excitement among the railroad employees, and conversations concerning the fortune in precious ore were common and careless.

After watching the heavy chest of ingots loaded into the boxcar, Briley and Kincaid decided that stealing the gold might offer a way out of their tiresome hunger and poverty. The boxcar door was slammed and locked, leaving no one inside to guard the shipment. After questioning one of the dockhands, Kincaid learned that only two men—the engineer and fireman—would be aboard the train on its journey to Wallula. On learning that the train would not depart until the following morning, the two men mounted their horses and rode westward along the tracks.

About an hour past sunrise, the engineer of the Rawhide Railroad train bound for Wallula pulled the brakes when he spotted a fallen tree lying across the tracks some distance ahead.

When the train finally ground to a stop a short distance from the tree, the engineer ordered the fireman to take an axe, cut up the obstructing oak, and remove it from the path. Just as the fireman leaped from the cab, a man wearing a bandanna across the lower half of his face climbed aboard the opposite side and pointed a pistol at the engineer. A masked partner rode out of the nearby trees, chased the surprised fireman into the woods, and continued toward one of the boxcars. After struggling with the lock for a few moments, he succeeded in breaking into the car and, locating the gold-filled chest, dragged it to the opening and pushed it outside onto the ground. Leaving the chest where it fell, he rode to the fallen tree, roped a stout limb, dallied the line around the saddle horn, and pulled the oak from the tracks.

At a wave from the second outlaw, the desperado guarding the engineer ordered the frightened man to get the train underway. As the locomotive chugged westward toward Wallula, the two masked outlaws broke open the trunk and loaded the ingots into their saddlebags. After mounting up, they quickly disappeared into the forest.

Once well away from the tracks, the riders paused while Kincaid unfolded a sheet of paper he removed from his shirt pocket. Examining the steamboat schedule, he found a list of departure times from the dock at Wallula. The two outlaws intended to book passage onto the steamer and, with the ingots, travel down the Columbia River to Portland where they hoped to convert the gold to cash and then flee into California. According to the schedule, the next boat would leave Wallula at noon the following day.

As the outlaws rode toward Wallula, their horses, unaccustomed to the extremely heavy loads they bore, grew weary and footsore, unable to maintain a consistent pace. Briley and Kincaid were forced to stop often and rest the animals, which brought on concern as to whether they would meet the steamboat on time. Eventually, the two train robbers hurried the animals along, whipping and spurring them when they slowed, but they were unsuccessful in coaxing any speed out of them.

When they finally arrived at Wallula, the two men discovered they had missed the boat by one hour. As they sat astride their mounts near the wharf, looking dejectedly toward the wide river, they were suddenly distracted by a man about forty yards away pointing at them and speaking excitedly to passersby. After a moment, Briley recognized the animated fellow as the engineer of the train they had robbed the previous day. Fearing they might be caught with the gold, the outlaws turned their exhausted mounts and rode back along the same trail they had followed into Wallula.

As the two outlaws fled from the town, the engineer sought the office of the local sheriff. Approximately three hours later, a posse composed of some fifteen men set out in pursuit of the bandits.

Stopping only briefly to allow their horses to water and graze, Briley and Kincaid were a few miles from Walla Walla when they spotted the posse gaining on them from about a mile away. Dismounting and unloading the saddlebags from their horses, they quickly dug a hole near a clump of bushes a few feet from the trail and buried the gold-filled saddlebags. Seconds later, they were spurring their horses toward town.

About a mile from Walla Walla, the two outlaws were overtaken by the lawmen. The bandits' horses, weakened from the long journey and the great weight they transported, were simply not strong enough to carry the riders to safety.

Briley and Kincaid were questioned by the posse members for about an hour, but they insisted they had no role in the train robbery. They presumed that, not finding any gold in their possession, the lawmen would simply let them go. Sometime later, they calculated, they would return to the place where they buried the saddlebags and retrieve them.

It was not to be. Tired and irritable from the long and arduous pursuit, the posse members decided to hang the two offenders on the spot, and moments later, Nate Briley and Jed Kincaid were swinging from a limb of a stout oak tree, nooses tightening around their necks and slowly choking the life from them.

During the return trip to Wallula, the posse members searched along the trail for some sign of burial of the stolen loot, but the location where the two bandits cached the ingots went unnoticed.

Somewhere just west of old Fort Walla Walla, the saddlebags filled with gold still lie just beneath the surface. This incredibly rich cache has tempted treasure hunters for decades but it has eluded the most persistent of them. The leather bags have no doubt rotted away since their burial, but the ingots remain, their value increased severalfold since they were hidden well over a century ago.

Indian Mission Gold Cache

During the 1890s, an elderly Indian chief regularly buried gold coins near the walls of St. Mary's Mission. The cache, which eventually represented his life's savings, is estimated to contain in excess of $60,000 at the face value of the hidden coins. The Indian, who died in 1918, never had the opportunity to retrieve his fortune, which today lies hidden just below the surface of the grassy yard of the old mission.

In 1889, a Catholic mission was founded on the Colville Indian Reservation in Ferry County, Washington. St. Mary's Indian Mission, as it was named, contained a convent, a school, and a small hospital, all established to minister to the area Indians. The mission was administered by Father Etienne de Rouge, a benevolent priest who easily gained the trust of his Indian charges. His church services were generally filled with the faithful converts from the reservation. Father de Rouge was loved and respected by the Indians because he allowed, even encouraged, them to retain many of their traditional customs and dress. Other, less tolerant, priests insisted the Indians abandon all manifestations of "savagery," and would not permit traditional dress, songs and chants, even language. Father de Rouge was aware of how important such things were to the Indians, and he realized if he was ever to gain their trust and accomplish his goals, he must show appreciation and respect for their native ways.

Among those who regularly attended church services at the mission was Chief Smitkin. Smitkin was the leader of the tribe for many years until the establishment of the mission. Though still revered by his people for his leadership and inspiration, Smitkin was comfortable with shedding the mantle of authority and responsibility and devoting his energies to operating a large cattle ranch on a parcel of land he was alloted.

Chief Smitkin was soon running six to seven hundred head of cattle on his range. Once a year, he would organize and lead a trail drive to deliver the beeves to a point on the Columbia River where they were loaded onto sturdy vessels and delivered to markets downriver as far as Portland. Smitkin always insisted that payment for his cattle be made in gold. As a result of his frugal lifestyle, Smitkin spent very little of his growing wealth, allowing it to accumulate in a small wooden box he kept under his bed.

In 1892, Smitkin, who could neither read, write, nor count, asked his wife's brother to count his gold for him. The brother-in-law, Albert Bailey, informed the old Indian his wealth totalled just over $20,000, assured him it was quite a bit of money, and encouraged him to deposit it in a bank where it would be safe. Smitkin thanked Bailey and returned the box of coins to its place under the bed and continued to add to it each time he sold more cattle.

As Smitkin's fortune increased, he grew concerned that he might be robbed. Unwilling to keep the money in the house any longer and distrustful of banks, the Indian decided to bury his gold in a secret location.

For reasons known only to himself, Smitkin cached his fortune in a shallow excavation near the walls of the mission church. Once or twice each year, he would take the proceeds of his most recent cattle sales and, during the dark of night, add them to his growing hoard. Smitkin continued to add gold coins to the cache until 1918, when he grew too old and infirm to continue ranching.

When Chief Smitkin was no longer able to walk or ride and was eventually confined to bed, he called in his son, Louis, and his brother-in-law, Albert Bailey. He told them both about burying his fortune near the mission and that when he died he wanted them to dig it up and divide it between themselves. The gold was buried, he said, near the farthest point touched by the evening shadows cast by the walls of the mission church. Weakened by the effort of speaking, and wracked by uncontrolled fits of coughing, Smitkin was unable to continue to provide specific directions. He bade his son and friend goodnight and asked them to return in the morning when he would tell them the exact location of the gold.

When the two men arrived at Smitkin's cabin the next day, however, the old man was dead, and with his passing went the secret to the location of the fortune in gold.

Undaunted, Louis Smitkin and Albert Bailey went to the mission early one evening and watched the progress of the evening shadows as they crept across the grassed yard eastward from the church. Just before the sun disappeared behind the western horizon, the two men scraped a line on the ground at the farthest extent of the irregular shadow. The line represented a sizable distance, but the two men, unable to wait for sunrise, began digging into the fertile ground. Throughout much of the night, the two excavated one hole after another in the dim light cast by an oil lantern. Finally, about two hours before dawn, young Smitkin and Bailey, both exhausted, gave up and went home.

The two men returned that same afternoon to resume their excavations, but the results were the same—they found no gold. For nearly a week, the men dug throughout the yard beside the church. Finally, Bailey suggested the supposed cache was a hoax and that the old Indian had never buried it at all. This accusation angered Louis Smitkin, harsh words were exchanged, and the two men abandoned the digging in anger.

Outside of family gatherings, Louis Smitkin refused to have anything to do with Albert Bailey, and the two men rarely spoke for the rest of their lives. Louis would occasionally return to the mission yard and excavate a new hole, but after many attempts and a like number of failures, he too was beginning to believe there might not be any gold after all—that perhaps Bailey had been correct in his assessment of the chief.

Many years later, when Louis Smitkin was an old man, he related the story of his father's buried gold to a new mission priest recently assigned to St. Mary's from California. He told the newcomer about his frustrating attempts to find the cache. When he related old Chief Smitkin's description of the gold being located "near the farthest point touched by the evening shadows," the priest fell deep into thought for a moment and then asked Louis if he knew the season of the year when his father originally buried the gold. Louis did not know and said as much to the priest, asking him why he would ask such a question. The priest went on to explain that, depending on the season the shadows cast by the setting sun will vary in length. If the part of the churchyard that was excavated was identified during the winter but old Chief Smitkin buried the gold in the summer, the distance between the apex of the shadows of the different seasons could be several feet.

Louis admired the priest's logic and decided it had merit. With his advanced age and growing infirmities, however, his enthusiasm for finding and recovering his father's fortune had waned, and while he often thought about renewing the search, he eventually decided against it.

The Smitkin fortune, long buried somewhere near the walls of the old church, is one of the least-known lost treasures in the state of Washington. Consequently, there have been few organized efforts to find the cache.

With the availability of today's highly effective and efficient metal detectors, there is a good possibility that a

persistent treasure hunter, skilled in the use of such machines, may locate the buried gold hidden in the ground
near the walls of the old mission.

Gold Cache of the Eccentric Salvor

People who lived nearby knew him only as Captain Johnson, and his first name has been lost to history. It was known he was a native of Scotland. Indeed, the old man spoke often and fondly of the country of his birth and schooling. It was also known that he had been a ship captain, for he often related his adventures of transporting shiploads of trade goods from Europe and the Atlantic seaboard around the tip of South America to the California missions and settlements. In 1848, Captain Johnson retired to a point of land on the extreme southwestern tip of Washington near Baker's Bay and settled on 640 acres he acquired there.

From the front porch of the mansion Johnson eventually constructed, he could look out over the mouth of the Columbia River. For hours, the former ship captain watched the comings and goings of vessels through his telescope. Part of him longed to return to the sea, but he regretfully realized he was too old for such things.

Johnson eventually married a Chinook Indian woman and fathered two sons. Though his family offered him joyous and satisfying distraction, Johnson continued to peer through his scope at the mighty ships entering and leaving the river. Latent desires to return to the sea constantly filled his thoughts.

Occasionally, Johnson would spot a ship arriving from the Pacific Ocean, the captain of which appeared to be confused as to which part of the river to enter. The retired captain would load his sons into a canoe and paddle out to the vessel with an offer to serve as a guide to safe passage. For this, Johnson was paid well in gold coins.

One afternoon, as Johnson was scanning the sea with his telescope, he saw a ship strike a dangerous rock outcrop. As seamen scrambled into lifeboats and rowed toward shore, the vessel sank beneath the waters.

Days later, Johnson gathered several of his wife's relatives, and together they rowed out to the site where the vessel had gone down. Employing the Indians as divers, Johnson managed to retrieve the ship's safe and its contents. This done, he informed the captain of the sunken vessel of the recovery. The captain, in turn, informed shipping line officials in New York. For his efforts, Johnson was paid a handsome sum, and after paying the divers, he was left with a large pouch filled with gold coins.

On three other occasions, Johnson organized the recovery of money and goods from other ships that sank in the area, and each time he was rewarded in gold coin.

Once, a vessel transporting a consignment of gold sank only a few miles from his home. The gold, which had been refined and formed into hundreds of slugs worth fifty dollars apiece, had come from the rich mines in California's Cascade Range. Johnson, with the help of his Indian divers, recovered the gold, worth millions of dollars. The mining company was all too happy to pay the extremely high salvage fee Johnson exacted, and when they did, the old captain found himself a rich man. The shipping company had paid him with some of the gold slugs.

Johnson became well known to residents of the area, and his neighbors spoke often about his skill as a salvor and a teller of fascinating tales of the sea. Though they regarded their neighbor as competent, they also considered him somewhat odd, even eccentric. Sometimes reclusive, he would lock himself inside his huge mansion, not even allowing his family entrance for days at a time. On the rare occasions he visited the nearby settlement of Astoria on the opposite shore of the Columbia River, he was usually seen talking to himself and wandering aimlessly among the many log buildings.

Johnson never placed his money in banks. He mistrusted these institutions and the people who managed them. Instead, the old captain preferred to bury his wealth on his own property. Johnson had a prescribed route through the woods that roughly circled his house and along which he would take walks several times a day. This narrow tree-lined lane he improvised through the forest brought the old man great pleasure, and he often spent hours clearing and cleaning it. When Johnson came into possession of a salvage fee or other significant income, he would place the money, always gold coins or slugs, into a leather pouch and carry it with him during one of his walks. Somewhere along the route, Johnson would bury the gold, adding the payment to his growing cache.

One day, Johnson's youngest son, George, quietly followed his father during one of his walks, staying well behind him on the trail. The youth watched with curiosity as the captain paused along a portion of the path that passed close to the edge of a steep slope that overlooked Baker's Bay. After looking about and assuming he was alone, the elder Johnson excavated a small hole and placed a pouch of gold coins into it. After covering the hole, he continued on his walk.

Several days later, George went to the site and dug up several of his father's gold coins, which he took home to play with. In later years, George recalled that inside the hole were several leather pouches, perhaps as many as twelve, and each was tightly packed with gold coins.

In 1857, Captain Johnson died suddenly. While he was returning from Astoria, his canoe overturned and he drowned. He passed away without leaving any directions to the location of his gold cache. Several months following his death, Johnson's wife decided to abandon the mansion and live with her relatives. As she made arrangements to leave, she searched throughout the big house for the fortune in gold she knew her husband possessed, but could find nothing. George, who at his young age was completely unaware of the importance of the gold coins he had found in the hole near the path, offered no insight into the location of his father's wealth.

In 1858, the Johnson property was sold to Isaac Whealdon. Whealdon, who saw promise in the rapidly growing settlement on the bay, operated a post office and store out of the old Johnson mansion. Originally, the settlement was called Pacific City and later changed to Unity. Today, the town is known as Ilwaco.

In 1863, Whealdon was interviewed by a newspaper reporter. During the conversation, Whealdon mentioned that men sometimes arrived at his property to search for gold coins they believed were buried by the previous owner. Never convinced a treasure was cached on his property, Whealdon let the men roam freely about his holdings searching for the gold, but no one ever found anything.

In 1882, a lone fisherman sailed to and camped on the shore of Baker's Bay for several days. When he was not trying his luck in the waters of the bay, the fisherman would explore about the area, sometimes collecting interesting stones. On one such trip, the fisherman was walking along the base of a steep incline made slick by recent rains and runoff. At the base of the slope, which was called Devil's Slide, he discovered a leather pouch half-buried in the mud. Picking up the pouch, he was surprised to find it quite heavy. But this reaction was nothing to the astonishment he experienced when he opened the pouch and found it filled with gold coins!

Ben Isaac Whealdon was the son of the man who purchased Johnson's property. On hearing the story of the fisherman's discovery, he theorized the pouch had eroded from Johnson's cache, which was likely located at or near the top of Devil's Slide. Young Whealdon, who had searched for the treasure himself, was convinced that many more gold-filled pouches could be found in the cache. Though he looked for the gold for years, Whealdon was never able to find the great hoard.

When George Johnson was in his sixties, he told of his childhood adventure of digging up some of the gold coins buried by his father. Decades had passed before George realized the value of the cache—and that the bulk of it probably still lay in the shallow hole near his late father's hiking path. George returned to the property many times and tried to find the gold, but to no avail. Forest growth had encroached onto the old hiking path, making it impossible to relocate.

Some who have studied the story of Captain Johnson's fortune believe the cache contains at least $20,000 in gold coins and slugs. Other researchers believe the $20,000 estimate is too conservative, and that the fortune likely approaches $60,000 in 1860 values. In any case, there is little doubt that an impressive treasure awaits the individual lucky enough to find the gold.

But Captain Johnson's gold may no longer lie in the secret cache above the bay. Some treasure hunters who have entered the old property and stood atop Devil's Slide are convinced the gold-filled pouches eroded out of the ground and were carried to the bottom of the slope to be deposited not far from the shore below on Baker's Bay. At some level beneath the surface of the accumulated dirt and debris at the bottom of the slide, they venture, the treasure will be found.

Treasure in the Well

Long Island is a northwest-southeast oriented wedge of land located in the southern reaches of Willapa Bay. Today, it is a wildlife refuge, but during the time when the nearby coastal area became attractive to white settlers, the island was home to only a few Indians and oyster fishermen. On the northern end of Long Island, an old, abandoned well lies somewhere on a piece of land once settled by John Lyon, an oyster fisherman and trapper. The exact location of the well remains a mystery to this day to the many who have searched for it, but its lure is powerful: at its bottom lies a fortune comprised of nearly 10,000 gold English sovereigns!

John Lyon lived with his Indian wife, Seika, not far from the shore on the northern tip of the island. Each morning the two walked the short path to the beach where the oyster boat was tied, pushed it out into the bay, and spent the day harvesting the shellfish from the rich and abundant beds, beds that, years later, were eventually depleted as settlement increased.

When the boat was heavy with oysters, Lyon would return Seika to shore and then row to the nearby settlements of Oysterville, Ilwaco, and Astoria, where he would peddle them to restaurants and stores. While Lyon was visiting these places, he would seek out and try his luck at card games, sometimes gambling away significant portions of his income. As often as he was able, Lyon purchased tickets for the English lotteries, tickets that were brought to the new settlements by the many trading vessels that plied the seas.

Seika disapproved of Lyon's gambling habits, scolding him often for what she perceived to be a foolish expenditure of money that came only from long, hard hours of work. A deeply religious woman, Seika often lectured the illiterate Lyon about gambling, occasionally quoting appropriate passages from the Bible. Sometimes Lyon, on returning home from one his trips and ripe with guilt from gambling, would confess his misdeeds to Seika. Following these revelations, he would suffer the scolding of his wife, scolding that would sometimes last for days. Seika regarded gambling as among the worst of the world's sins and was convinced her husband would burn in hell because of his weakness for it.

During a subsequent trip to Oysterville, Lyon learned he had won one of the English lotteries and that his prize was to be 10,000 golden sovereigns. His winnings, he learned, were soon to be shipped from England and delivered to his home. Elated at his good fortune, Lyon nevertheless grew concerned on his return journey to Long Island. He feared Seika would fly into a rage about what he perceived only as good luck. He finally decided he would simply keep his winnings a secret from her.

It was not to be. Several weeks later and unknown to Lyon, the 10,000 gold sovereigns were dropped off at Oysterville by a British merchant vessel, packed into leather bags, and delivered to his home on the island. When the courier dropped off the lottery winnings at Lyons cabin, Seika could barely control her anger and demanded to know why he continued to indulge in the horrible sin of gambling. An argument raged into the night, and Seika finally told Lyon she was leaving, never to return. When he begged her to remain and promised to do anything to keep her, she told him that he must unburden himself of his ill-gotten gains. Lyon promised he would.

Two days later, the oyster fisherman found an ideal place to hide his fortune. He decided to tie the gold-filled saddlebags to a stout cord and hang them in the well. As his wife never visited the well, Lyon felt certain she would never learn of his unusual hiding place. Sometimes, when Seika was not around, Lyon would walk to the well, pull up the suspended bags of money, and count the sovereigns.

Late one afternoon, Lyon went to the well to look at his money and spotted an owl perched on the wall. To Seika's tribe, the owl was regarded as an omen of bad luck, sometimes even death. Frightened, Lyon turned and walked back up the path away from the well.

Several days later, Lyon returned once again to the well but found the same owl perched in the same location. Convinced bad luck was to soon descend upon him, he ran back to his cabin.

A week later, Seika was stricken with a strange illness. Convinced that the appearance of the owl was somehow connected to his wife's sickness, Lyon suffered for days from an oppressive feeling of guilt, believing that his sinful gambling was responsible for the malady that affected his wife.

For two weeks, Seika suffered from fever and delirium. Finally she died, and the inconsolable Lyon cried for days. He could not bring himself to harvest the oysters and spent hours at a time grieving over Seika's grave.

Eventually, Lyon decided he must leave the island and go live someplace far away, far from the bad memories that plagued him. He went to the well to retrieve his fortune, money that would enable him to begin a new life elsewhere.

On arriving at the well this time, Lyon again encountered the same owl and decided that the gold sovereigns were somehow cursed, that they would bring him nothing but bad luck. Packing only a few belongings, Lyon fled the island, leaving the coins dangling in the well. He fled to Astoria, and from there struck out eastward on foot along a well-used wagon trail and was never seen in the area again.

For years, Lyon's deserted homesite remained undisturbed. After it had been abandoned for several years, an occasional fisherman or homesteader would occupy the site for a time, but no one remained long. One year, following weeks of steady rain, a mud slide roared down the slope behind Lyon's old cabin, destroying the log structure and covering the old well.

Years later, an elderly prospector arrived on Long Island and spent several days wandering around the old homesite as if he were searching for something. When nearby residents inquired about his activities, he explained that he had met Lyon in an Idaho mining camp months earlier. There, the former fisherman told of hiding the 10,000 golden sovereigns in the well located on his property. Unfortunately, the old prospector could never find the well under the mud-slide debris.

In 1965, a state game and fish employee visited the island on a special game census assignment and spent several days in the area of the old Lyon homesite. He observed that recent rains had eroded a significant amount of earth and debris from portions of a slope and an old, dilapidated cabin. Not far away, the state employee discovered what he believed was the shaft to an old well. As he searched about, he caught the glint of a shiny object partially buried in the ground. On picking it up, he was astonished to discover it was a golden English sovereign! Thinking there might be others nearby, he dug into the ground for nearly an hour but found nothing. Days later, his work completed, he left the island, never to return.

Little did the visitor to Long Island realize that, under his feet, probably only a few inches from where he stood, 9,999 more gold coins lay buried in what was left of the old well.

Port Discovery Gold

Somewhere in the sands of Port Discovery Bay, located on the northern coast of the Olympic Peninsula, lies a wooden chest nearly filled with gold coins, a fortune stolen from a British Columbia railroad company and buried during the subsequent flight of the thief. It is estimated that this chest contains approximately one million dollars' worth of coins at today's value, an incredible wealth that has attracted treasure hunters by the score to the region. To date, however, this fascinating fortune has never been recovered, and some say the location where it was buried is now several feet under water.

During one summer night in 1864, an employee of a British Columbia railway on Vancouver Island who was entrusted with the company payroll disappeared, taking an estimated $60,000 in gold coins. Unknown to railroad authorities at the time, the thief placed the gold in a stout wooden chest, loaded it into a boat, and paid a local Indian to transport him across the Strait of Juan de Fuca in his boat. The Indian, whose identity was learned several days later, told investigators that he transported his passenger, along with the heavy trunk, to a deserted beach at Port Discovery Bay, arriving shortly after midnight. After dropping off his passenger and cargo, the Indian immediately started on his return trip to Vancouver Island. As he negotiated his craft away from the shore, he claimed he watched his passenger scoop out a large hole in the sand, presumably intending to bury the chest. For payment, the Indian was given a handful of gold coins which were later identified as being among those stolen from the railway safe.

After burying the gold-filled chest on the beach, the thief hiked a short distance inland. Around dawn, he came upon a small farm, approached the log cabin residence, and asked to borrow a horse to travel to nearby Port Townsend. The homesteader, a man named John F. Tukey, cheerfully provided a mount and bade his visitor a good journey.

At Port Townsend, the payroll thief booked passage to Olympia on a ship that carried supplies to the many settlements and outposts found on the islands and peninsulas of Puget Sound. Meanwhile, railroad officials discovered the missing payroll and alerted law enforcement representatives.

Aboard the Olympia-bound ship, the payroll thief, assuming he was entirely safe and free from prosecution in the United States, began bragging about stealing the $60,000 from the railway. The captain of the vessel, however, immediately locked the man into a cabin, changed course, and delivered him to authorities at Vancouver, British Columbia.

Though questioned for days and ultimately sentenced to prison, the thief never revealed the location of the buried gold. Years later when he was released from his incarceration, detectives followed him for several weeks in the hope he might return to Port Discovery Bay to dig up the treasure. Fearing the stolen gold would bring him more bad luck, the ex-prisoner spent a month or two traveling around northern California and then finally departed for Texas, where he moved in with a relative. He never returned to Washington.

Homesteader Tukey, in relating the story of the buried treasure years later, told of a visit from a contingent of Canadian lawmen following the robbery. While Tukey watched, the group undertook a search of his property for the missing payroll, eventually working their way down to the beach at Port Discovery Bay. Tukey stated that the members of the recovery party manifested no serious interest in the gold and merely went through the motions of a search. Eventually they returned to Canada empty-handed.

Tukey eventually decided to search for the treasure himself, and over the next several years he would sometimes wander around his property and the beach examining likely hiding places. By the time Tukey passed away in 1912, however, he had never found as much as a single coin.

By the mid-1940s, the tale of the buried payroll of gold coins was being told throughout the Pacific Northwest, and soon treasure hunters were swarming all over the old Tukey property. In 1946, a man named Philip Bailey purchased the Tukey homestead. In 1948, Bailey was approached by three Seattle men who requested permission to search for the treasure. Bailey agreed to allow the trio to hunt for the gold-filled chest and negotiated the rights to fifty percent of anything that might be recovered.

For reasons unknown to Bailey or anyone else, the men concentrated their search near the old Tukey cabin and neglected the beach altogether. Researchers have estimated the chest filled with $60,000 in gold coins would have weighed around 250 pounds, far too heavy for a single individual to have dragged so far inland. After weeks of searching and finding nothing, the Seattle men finally gave up and departed.

In 1949, Bailey allowed one of his neighbors on the property to conduct a search with a metal detector. After weeks of looking for the gold and excavating dozens of holes, he, like the men from Seattle, finally gave up and abandoned the quest.

Over the years, Bailey was approached by dozens more treasure hunters, all of whom claimed the gold was buried somewhere near the site of the old cabin. None were successful.

Today, most researchers who have thoroughly studied the tale are convinced the chest full of gold coins was never transported any farther than the edge of the beach near where the thief was dropped off by the Indian. It has also been suggested that the region where it is assumed the thief landed has long since been eroded away by continuous wave action. If true—and the likelihood is great—the chest probably lies below the maximum tidal advance. Professional treasure hunters concur that an underwater search with specialized metal detectors might yield the location of the gold-filled chest. If the treasure is found, recovery efforts could be facilitated with the use of scuba equipment. And at today's gold values, it is estimated at least one million dollars awaits anyone fortunate enough to make the discovery.

Lost Gold Cache of
James Scarborough

James Scarborough signed up to be a sailor on the barkentine *Isabella* in September 1829. As this multimasted sailing vessel owned by the Hudson Bay Company untied from and departed the British docks, caught the wind, and plied the waters of the broad Atlantic Ocean, Scarborough had no inkling he would someday be associated with one of the greatest lost treasure mysteries of America's Pacific Northwest.

Born into and raised by an English family in Essex, all Scarborough ever wanted was to abandon the city and sail the world's oceans. Someday, he hoped, he would command a fleet of his own ships and build a sailing and merchant empire unrivaled by any other in the world.

It was not to be. Following the long and sometimes stormy transatlantic voyage, the incredibly rough and dangerous passage around South America's Cape Horn, and the seemingly interminable journey up the west coasts of North and South America, Scarborough wearied of the sea and vowed to seek his fortune on land. When the *Isabella* ran aground on a sandbar at the mouth of the Columbia River, Scarborough was almost relieved. With the ship wrecked beyond repair, he and several shipmates sought refuge on the nearby shore. With solid ground now beneath his feet, Scarborough agreed to remain a sometime employee of the Hudson Bay Company while developing his own business on land. During the next twenty years, Scarborough occasionally captained trading vessels for his employer, but he was happiest when ensconced in the home he constructed on the 640-acre parcel of land he claimed and settled not far from the present-day town of Chinook overlooking Baker's Bay near the mouth of the Columbia River.

In 1843, Scarborough wed a Chinook Indian and took her to his home on Scarborough Hill, the name by which this gentle and rolling promontory is known today. When Scarborough retired from the Hudson Bay Company in 1850, his great passion was his homestead, and he spent many hours merely walking the winding trails through the wooded property.

Employing several members of the Chinook Indian tribe, Scarborough eventually established a thriving fishing business. After catching and packing salted salmon into barrels, he shipped them regularly to a broker in England. For payment, Scarborough would accept nothing but gold, and it had to be in the form of ingots or slugs.

Over the years, it is estimated Scarborough's fishing business netted him between $60,000 and $100,000, all in gold—and all buried somewhere on his property. According to his widow and descendants, Scarborough lived off the land and, save the spare wages he paid his Indian workers, spent little of the income he derived from his fishing enterprise. Instead, he cached it in a secret location near his home.

James Scarborough died in February 1855. Except for his wife, Scarborough never revealed the location of his gold cache to anyone. After his death, relatives and neighbors tried to find his treasure over the years, but none were successful. Scarborough's Chinook wife, a charming woman to whom he had given the name Elizabeth, refused to reveal any details about the location of the gold. Like many Indians in the area, she believed buried wealth, especially gold, was intended only for the person who hid it. If another were to retrieve the gold, a curse would be placed on that person and he and his family would die needlessly.

In 1864, the federal government decided the region containing much of Scarborough's property was important to the defense of the Columbia River and purchased the land for a military base. Fort Columbia was constructed in 1894 and manned until the mid-1940s. Today, Scarborough's original homestead is part of the Fort Columbia State Heritage Area. This pleasant park contains a handsome museum, and in it hangs a painting of Captain James Scarborough, hailed as the first white settler in the region.

While tourism is the principal attraction in this area today, a few have not forgotten Scarborough's cache of gold ingots. Up until her death in the early 1900s, Scarborough's widow was regularly visited by treasure hunters who sought information on the valuable cache, but she remained silent.

During the early 1930s, a construction crew working west of the town of Chinook was leveling a hillside in preparation for construction of the Ocean Beach Highway to Fort Columbia. One of the machinery operators paused while bulldozing away a portion of a low hill when he caught the gleam of a rectangular object on the ground. On investigation, he found it to be a gold ingot! Where it was unearthed and how far it was pushed by the bulldozer before being discovered he could only guess. Work was stopped for three days while searchers sought more of the gold, but none was found.

After the bulldozer operator's experience was reported in a Tacoma newspaper, many familiar with the Scarborough treasure believed it must be located somewhere near the new highway. Within a few days, dozens of treasure hunters roamed the right-of-way searching for the cache. Since that time, seekers of the Scarborough treasure have been seen regularly scanning the roadsides with metal detectors. None were successful, but a curious discovery was made in 1988 that led many to believe the treasure was still there, still hidden on the old Scarborough property.

A family from Indiana, on an outing to the Pacific Northwest, paused at a picnic area along the Ocean Beach Highway to prepare lunch and shoot some photographs. While Claire Young prepared lunch, her husband, Brad, accompanied by two sons, six and ten years of age, walked into the nearby woods. Young wanted to photograph some squirrels playing in the treetops and the boys laughed and frolicked while romping through the forest.

While attempting to find a suitable camera angle relative to the afternoon sunlight filtering through the tree canopy, Young was interrupted by the chattering of his six-year-old, who was trying to gain his attention. When Young finally looked down from his task, the boy showed him a circular object he had found close by. At first, the object, being roughly circular, appeared to be a coin, but after cleaning some of the dirt from it, Young found it to be only a faceless slug. When Young scraped at the surface with his penknife, he was startled to discover it was composed of solid gold!

After asking his son where he had found the item, Young followed the youth into a nearby cluster of trees. Once in the denser forest, however, the boy became disoriented and was unable to retrace the path he had taken only minutes earlier. The three searched throughout this portion of the woods for nearly an hour but were unable to find any more of the gold slugs.

Is James Scarborough's lost gold cache located somewhere near the Ocean Beach Highway, just a short distance into the adjacent woods? It would appear so, and it may only be a matter of time before some lucky hiker or treasure hunter stumbles onto it.

Recent Gold Nugget Discoveries in Kittitas County

While traveling throughout the Pacific Northwest during the summer of 1988, I delighted in occasional visits with several well-known modern-day prospectors and placer miners. During the course of our conversations, I found many of them excited about relatively recent discoveries of impressively large gold nuggets in Swauk Creek, a Kittitas County stream.

Kittitas County is located in central Washington. The majority of the area lies between the Wenatchee Mountains to the northwest and the Columbia River to the east. During the early settlement of this region, most of the major streams and tributaries were sites for significant placer mining. One of the placer miners I visited with displayed several nuggets he had recently taken from the area, each the size of a grape or larger. Other miners reported similar discoveries. Surprisingly, none of the nuggets came directly out of the creek itself—they were all dug from the rows of waste gravel left over from turn-of-the-century mining operations!

Swauk Creek flows out of the Wenatchee Mountains. Exposed portions of the Wenatchees are composed, in large part, of granite, some of which has long been known to be ore-bearing. The Swauk, a swiftly flowing tributary to the Yakima River, transports a substantial quantity of eroded debris from these mountains, and among this fluvial load are often extraordinary amounts of gold. So much gold was found in this stream during the 1870s and 1880s that a major placer mining operation organized by a California syndicate was eventually established on the creek during the latter part of the century.

When the mining company arrived at Swauk Creek, agents for the organization immediately bought up claims and established, for that time, a very sophisticated dredging operation in an attempt to recover as much gold as possible. Knowing that gold, because of its relative density, seeks the lowest level, the idea was to get to the bedrock of the stream and glean the ore from the cracks and fissures where it commonly gathers. In the attempt to reach bedrock, however, tons of overlying gravel were removed and piled along the banks and edges of the creek, gravel that was ultimately found to contain quantities of gold. During the gravel removal process, much of the rock was subjected to screening and sieving and some gold was successfully retrieved. A great deal of it, apparently, went undetected.

After dredging several miles of Swauk Creek and harvesting all of the bedrock gold believed to lie there, the mining company simply shut down and abandoned the area, leaving the unsightly piles of gravel to the elements.

Scenic State Highway 97 winds northward from Interstate 90 toward the town of Liberty, and for a few miles along its course, the roadway parallels Swauk Creek. It is possible to view the piles and rows of gravel left over from these early mining activities from the window of an automobile.

Sometime during the 1940s, a carload of vacationers pulled off Highway 97 and the occupants got out and explored around the old abandoned rows of gravel. One of the travelers picked a large, gleaming stone from one of the piles and, fascinated with its brilliance and hue, placed it in her pocket. Weeks later, she showed the rock to someone knowledgeable about minerals and learned it was a gold nugget, worth approximately four hundred dollars!

Word soon spread around the region about the gold that could be found in the old gravel piles, and soon people were driving from hundreds of miles away to prospect among the old dredging waste for the ore. Remarkably, thousands of dollars' worth of gold was easily reclaimed from the deposits over a period of several years.

Time passed, and the excitement relative to searching for and finding gold among the Swauk Creek mining waste abated somewhat. Once the tourists and the weekend miners abandoned the region, however, professional placer miners moved in. During the 1950s, three men regularly worked the diggings, and as they systematically prospected and dug into the piles of waste gravel, they routinely came away with pouches filled with gold nuggets, some of them quite large. One single nugget discovered by a miner named Nathan Goodheart was valued at $1,100! In time, there were as many as eighteen miners working in the gravel rows.

Why were so many large and valuable gold nuggets left in the waste gravel? The answer, according to some of the men currently mining the waste, has to do with the screening and sieving process employed by the early placer mining company. The rotating screen process used for sifting out fine sands, gravels, and small gold nuggets rejected virtually anything larger than a grape. As it turned out, Swauk Creek apparently contained thousands of gold nuggets of relatively large size, large enough to be rejected during the screening operation. Many of those nuggets were unknowingly tossed into the piles of waste from which they are being mined today.

A visit to the creek with one of the miners offered insight into the gold retrieval process. Filling two metal buckets with waste gravel, the miner carried them about ten paces to the creek where he expertly washed the rocks, eventually swirling some of the smaller debris around the bottom of the placer pan. Three hours of concentrated labor yielded several gold nuggets—six in all—and each one nearly as large as the end segment of my little finger.

This unique mining operation, rather than having a questionable effect on the local environment like many excavation processes, has been an ecological boon to the region's stream ecology. "Not only are we finding gold in these deposits," stated one of the miners, "but in the process of removing it we are gradually replacing the gravels back into the stream from where they came."

These placer miners remain sensitive to and concerned about the natural environment while at the same time making a decent profit.

Columbia River Payroll Gold

John Ledbetter was never a man to take orders. Fired from one job after another in his hometown of Pittsburgh, Pennsylvania, Ledbetter loaded his wife, Mary, two daughters, and all of their belongings into an ox-drawn wagon and drifted westward in search of a new life.

Ledbetter found employment at sawmills, loading docks, tanneries, and railroad-tie factories, but after a few weeks at each job, he grew irritated at having to take orders and quit.

Scant hours after joining a Washington-bound wagon train in St. Louis, Ledbetter and the wagonmaster fell into a disagreement relative to the Pennsylvanian's place in the line. The two men briefly exchanged punches before being separated by other travelers, but their animosity for one another remained heated during the ensuing weeks on the trail.

Several weeks later, as the wagon train negotiated a steep descent through a mountain pass in Idaho, Ledbetter and the wagonmaster fought once again, this time over the correct way to attach safety lashes to the wagons on the downhill slope.

Once the train finally arrived in the gentle rolling foothills on the western side of the mountains, Ledbetter angrily announced he was leaving and intended to complete the journey to the coast on his own. Several members of the wagon train begged Ledbetter to consider the safety of his wife and children and pleaded with him not to go. Not to be dissuaded, Ledbetter cursed the stupidity of the wagonmaster and all who would continue to follow him, and whipped his oxen toward a northwesterly course away from the main trail.

Two weeks later—and after two wagon breakdowns—John Ledbetter was driving his wagon along a landscape, unmarked by trails, in eastern Washington. The desertlike environment yielded very little water, and the oxen were showing the strain of continued travel with reduced forage.

Days passed, and the Ledbetter wagon eventually arrived at what is now called the McCarteney River in present-day Douglas County. The trickle of water in the stream was sufficient for watering the animals and filling the casks, and here the family rested for three days and nights.

Refreshed from the extended stop, the Ledbetters grew slightly more optimistic about the remainder of their journey as they followed the McCarteney River downstream, hoping it would eventually lead them to the Columbia River.

After traveling southwestward for an hour on the floodplain of the stream, Ledbetter spotted a man lying on the ground about one hundred yards ahead. As the wagon creaked up to the prone form, the man rolled over and tried to rise only to fall back into a heap atop his bulging saddlebags.

After pulling the stranger into the shade of the wagon, Mary Ledbetter ministered to him while John bent to examine the saddlebags. A moment later, he called out for his family to join him, and when they arrived at his side he was pointing to nearly one hundred pounds of gold coins!

The stranger was too weak to walk and there was no room for him in the wagon, so Ledbetter decided to set up camp on the spot, hoping for a quick recovery.

That evening, after the meal was completed and the light from the campfire flickered low, the stranger regained consciousness and began to babble incoherently. Exhausted from his efforts after only a few minutes, he quieted down and glanced around, frightened eyes probing the darkness. On spotting Ledbetter, he asked him if he was the law. When Ledbetter replied he was not, the stranger reached out his arms and begged to be taken to Portland. When Ledbetter asked why, he related an amazing story.

The stranger, who said his name was Ridley, said he and three other men had robbed a freight wagon one week earlier. The wagon was traveling from Wenatchee to a mining company in a remote part of the Cascade Range when it was stopped by the outlaws. The robbers, intent on stealing some mining equipment to resell, were surprised to discover the wagon was transporting a huge payroll of gold coins bound for the mines. Only three of the highwaymen had saddlebags strapped to their mounts, and into these the gold was placed. While the fourth bandit continued searching the wagon, a party of six miners rode into view around a bend in the road, discerned that a robbery was taking place, and immediately opened fire on the bandits. The outlaw in the wagon was killed instantly, a bullet through his head. Another was wounded in the chest and knocked from his horse. The remaining two outlaws leaped onto their mounts and sped away, with Ridley riding back down the trail while the other charged into the cover of the forest. Just before the two separated, they agreed to meet in Portland.

For two days, Ridley barely stayed ahead of three men who followed in pursuit. During that time he ate nothing and only stopped briefly to water his horse and himself. On the third day, the pursuers had abandoned the chase. Ridley, relieved at his escape, spurred his exhausted mount down a narrow trail when the animal, undernourished and weak from carrying rider and one hundred pounds of gold, suddenly collapsed and died. Frustrated but with no other alternative, Ridley slung the heavy saddlebags across one shoulder and staggered down the trail.

Hungry and tired, the outlaw carried his share of the loot several miles over the next three days. After fording the shallow McCarteney River during the night, the exhausted and starving Ridley finally gave out and dropped to the ground, unconscious. It was several hours later when Ledbetter found the outlaw lying on the floodplain.

The following morning after starting a cookfire, Ledbetter went to wake Ridley and discovered the man was dead. After burying the outlaw and loading the gold-filled saddlebags into the wagon, Ledbetter and his family resumed their journey.

After two days of slow and difficult travel, the Ledbetters arrived at the banks of the Columbia River just downstream from the McCarteney River confluence. The Columbia did not appear to be too deep, and Ledbetter decided to drive across. Several yards out into the stream, however, the surging current buffeted the top-heavy wagon such that Ledbetter was concerned it might turn over. Fearing for the safety of his family, he turned the oxen and retreated to the eastern shore.

Ledbetter decided to set up camp on the floodplain for a few days and wait for the water to recede enough to allow for safe passage. While encamped, the Ledbetters were joined by two more wagonloads of travelers, also on their way to the coast.

After studying the stream, one of the newcomers announced that it could be crossed if the wagons carried lighter loads. With that, some goods were dumped from each, and Ledbetter watched closely as they crossed safely to the opposite shore.

Deciding to follow this example, Ledbetter and his wife began removing objects from their overloaded wagon—first a large wooden chest, then a stout oak bureau. Finally, Ledbetter suggested they might as well bury the saddlebag full of gold nearby and return for it after getting his wagon and family across the river. Selecting what he deemed an appropriate location, Ledbetter excavated a hole approximately two feet deep, deposited the bag, and covered it over. Before leaving, he placed several large rocks atop the cache.

About an hour later, the Ledbetter wagon arrived on the other side of the Columbia River. With both driver and animals completely exhausted from the crossing, Ledbetter decided to set up camp for the night on the first flood terrace and, using one of the oxen, return for the gold the next morning.

During the night, however, the Ledbetters were awakened by the booming thunder of a great storm moving across the Wenatchee Mountains and dropping sheets of rain over a large area. By sunrise, Ledbetter looked down upon a flooded, surging river that had swollen its banks and spilled over onto the floodplains on both sides. Ledbetter watched in awe as the swift current carried huge trees uprooted by the torrent from somewhere upstream.

For nearly a week, the Ledbetters remained camped on the terrace waiting for the floodwaters to recede. Finally, when he was certain it would be safe to cross, John Ledbetter rode one of the oxen across the river to retrieve the gold coins.

When Ledbetter reached the eastern side he became disoriented. Nothing was the same! Certain he was standing on the exact spot where he and Mary had deposited the furniture, he looked around and could find nothing, no trace. Everything had been swept away by the floodwaters. Walking over to where he was certain the gold was buried, Ledbetter was dismayed to discover the heavy rocks he placed atop the cache were also gone. Believing he was at the correct location, Ledbetter began to excavate but soon realized it was the wrong place. After digging about a dozen holes nearby, Ledbetter grew worried he might never find the gold. For the next two days, growing increasingly frustrated, he dug well over one hundred holes in search of the fortune. Eventually, he conceded that he would likely never find the coins and, crossing the Columbia River for the final time in his life, hitched the team of oxen to the wagon and continued on to the coast.

John Ledbetter never came back to search for the gold, but he told his story to others. Over the years, it is estimated hundreds have dug into the sandy eastern floodplain of the Columbia River downstream from the McCarteney River confluence in search of the payroll gold, but no discovery of the fabulous cache has ever been reported.

Some claim the Columbia River floodwaters washed the coins away and scattered them downstream. Others believe that continued flooding and sediment deposition actually covered the cache with an extra one or two feet of debris. Geographers who study the hydrological goings-on of rivers and streams maintain that the floodplain environment here would be more conducive to preserving the cache rather than removing it.

The possibility that this little-known yet incredibly rich treasure is still buried somewhere in the eastern floodplain of the Columbia River in Douglas County is quite good. Equipped with sophisticated detection gear, some fortunate treasure hunter may someday recover what is likely worth well over a million dollars in vintage gold coins.

Lost Skeleton Gold Mine

During the late 1930s in southwestern Washington, miner Frank Smits was working very hard for long hours trying to make a living digging cinnabar from the ground near Mount Adams. Mount Adams, a Cascade Range peak rising 12,276 feet into the clouds, was a favorite prospecting site for the energetic and determined Smits, and during the previous dozen years he had found gold, silver, and other minerals, but never in quantities that generated significant profit.

Cinnabar yields mercury, and Smits believed he would eventually become a rich man if he could remove enough of the rock and transport it to the processor with whom he had made an agreement. To facilitate the speed and efficiency of transportation of the cinnabar from the mine to the refinery, Smits explored throughout the area in search of a shorter route with less gradient.

Smits had many years' experience as a miner, a mining engineer, and an architect. While considerably short of the fortune he hoped to someday find, he still managed to provide a good living for his family. The cinnabar deposit, he concluded, would eventually make him a wealthy man.

With thoughts of the future and a potential life of luxury for himself, his wife, and his children, Smits crisscrossed the terrain in and around the foothills of Mount Adams in search of an appropriate route.

At some point during his surveying, Smits spotted a cave opening at the base of a cliff that loomed a short distance from the seldom-used dirt road he traveled. Curious about such things, he decided to investigate.

After stepping inside the opening of the cave, Smits could plainly see the cavern extended deep into the side of the mountain. Fashioning a crude torch from some nearby grasses, he penetrated deeper into the darkness. Nearly one hundred yards from the opening he came upon a rickety wooden ladder that extended downward to a lower level. His meager torch cast insufficient light to illuminate the bottom. Deciding to return on the next morning with appropriate lighting, Smits crawled back out of the cave.

The following day, miner Smits entered the cave wearing his miner's helmet to which was attached a carbide lamp. In addition, he carried two flashlights. After reaching the wooden ladder, he cautiously descended nearly thirty feet and found himself standing on a gravel bar next to an underground stream. A few paces away, Smits spotted a sluice box of ancient vintage.

Exploring along the stream, which ranged in width from three to eight feet, Smits eventually came to a recess in a portion of the cavern that apparently served as living quarters for the miner of yore who had panned for gold here. In the recess he found an old stove, some bent metal pots, a shovel and other tools, a pistol, and a muzzle loader. As he gazed upon these items, Smits pondered the incredible amount of effort it must have taken to transport the stove through the cavern, lower it down to this level, and move the cumbersome object to this location.

Not far from this cluster of utensils and weapons, Smits spotted a wooden bed made from scrap material. As he approached it, Smits was startled to discover the skeletal remains of man lying atop it. The man had evidently been dead for a long time, as his skin was stretched tightly over his bones and the remnants of his clothing lay in rotted tatters among the blankets.

At the foot of the bed Smits spied a wooden trunk, and to this he directed his attention in the hope of finding some clue as to the identity of the dead man. Using the light of his lamp, he read through numerous documents, encountered several books, including a Bible, and examined three different photographs of a woman with two small children.

In a heavy manila envelope, Smits found some papers containing the seal of the State of Virginia. In another envelope, he discovered a legal title to some property in Washington state. The document was more than fifty years old and contained the name Isaac N. Huffman. Smits concluded this must be the name of the dead man.

Smits then turned his attention to the stream running along the floor of this level of the cavern. Because Huffman had obviously gone to a great deal of trouble moving into this remote part of the cavern, Smits was convinced he must have experienced some success at panning gold from the streambed. Though Smits spent almost two hours sifting through the stream gravels, he could find no evidence of gold in the dim light of his failing lantern.

Finally, after spending nearly a half-day in the dark cavern, Smits returned to the sunshine and fresh air of the mountainside. Though he thought of the dead Huffman during the ensuing years, Smits concentrated his attention on mining cinnabar.

Twelve years later, Frank Smits found himself in the Thurston County courthouse in Olympia checking on the availability of some mineral claims in various parts of the state. Though his dreams of becoming rich from the mining of cinnabar had not come to fruition, the ever-optimistic Smits remained active and hopeful and continued to pursue leads on deposits of other valuable minerals.

Seated in a musty room with a stack of ledgers in front of him, Smits mentioned to the nearby clerk that he was interested in securing some mineral rights on some land adjacent to the west slope of Mount Adams. Without looking up from his work, the clerk replied that the specific location mentioned was probably close to the lost Huffman gold mine.

Smits absorbed the comment without response and continued with his examination of the books. It was several hours later, during dinner at home, that it suddenly occurred to him that Huffman was the name on the documents found in the possession of the dead man he discovered in the cave a dozen years earlier!

The next morning, Smits was back at the courthouse seeking an audience with the clerk. After explaining the reason for his interest in Isaac N. Huffman, Smits was taken to a tiny room referred to as "the archives" and stood by while the clerk searched through several volumes of bound documents.

Finally, the clerk pointed to several entries in one book that showed Huffman, in 1882, had filed a claim on a parcel of land near the area where Smits found the cave. Working throughout most of the morning, the clerk occasionally recalled tales he had heard over the years of the lost gold mine and related them to Smits. Eventually, he produced several more documents that showed a man named Huffman had brought quantities of gold ore to Olympia on several different occasions and was paid a total of $44,000! Gold, Smits suspected, that was mined from the streambed that lay at the lower level of the mysterious cavern he had chanced upon twelve years earlier!

After listening to more of the clerk's stories, Smits left the courthouse firmly convinced that gold, and likely a large amount of it, lay deep within the cavern that housed the skeleton of Isaac N. Huffman. If Huffman, using the primitive gold-mining equipment that was evident in the cavern, was able to convert his mineral harvest into $44,000 in 1882 values, then the value of the gold likely remaining could be staggering. Smits was determined to mine it, but the first order of business for the miner was to relocate the entrance to the cave.

Several weeks passed before Smits was able to return to the slopes of Mount Adams, but once there he threw himself into the effort of searching for the entrance to what he began referring to as the Lost Skeleton Gold Mine.

Driving along the trail he believed passed close to the cliff containing the cave opening, Smits was struck by how different the countryside looked, how much it had changed since his last visit to the region. Fires had cleared away portions of the forest, but worst of all, landslides had changed the character of the cliff face and adjacent slopes.

In the region where he believed the mouth of the cave was located, he could see evidence of a relatively recent rock slide, with tons of debris completely covering the lower portion of the cliff face to a thickness of twenty to forty feet.

After more passes through the area and double-checking his log of twelve years earlier, Smits gradually grew convinced the entrance to the Lost Skeleton Gold Mine had been was completely blocked by the recent slide.

Six weeks later, Smits was back at the approximate location of the cave entrance with a truckload of dynamite and two helpers. After setting off a series of charges among the piles of rock-slide debris, Smits not only was unsuccessful in removing a significant amount of material from the entrance, he also managed to generate even more slides from above. The additional deposits of fallen rock, along with complaints from owners of adjacent property, forced Smits to abandon his project.

Reentry into the Lost Skeleton Gold Mine was never accomplished, and today, the dark opening to the cavern remains hidden beneath tons of rubble.

Selected References

Gresser, Donald. "Lost Cave of Gold." *True Treasure*. Winter 1967.

Henson, Michael Paul. "Oodles of Oregon Loot!" *Lost Treasure*. February 1991.

————. "Oregon Gold!" *Lost Treasure*. January 1992.

————. "Washington Treasures." *Lost Treasure*. August 1992.

————. "Washington Wealth!" *Lost Treasure*. April 1991.

Hult, Ruby El. *Lost Mines and Treasures of the Pacific Northwest*. Portland: Binfords & Mont, 1957.

————. *Treasure Hunting Northwest*. Portland: Binfords & Mont, 1971.

Jameson, W.C. "Crater Lake Gold." *Lost Treasure*. July 1994.

————. "Indian Mission Gold Cache." *Lost Treasure*. May 1994.

————. "Scottish Lord's Buried Treasure Chest." *Lost Treasure*. September 1994.

————. "Skeletons and Gold Nuggets." *Lost Treasure*. October 1994.

Kelly, Bill. "Exclusive Clues To John Turnow's Cache." *Lost Treasure*. July 1993.

Latham, John H. *Famous Lost Mines of the Old West*. Conroe, Texas: True Treasure Publications, Inc., 1971.

LeGaye, E.S. *Treasure Anthology*. Houston, Texas: Western Heritage Press, 1973.

Lovelace, Leland. *Lost Mines and Hidden Treasure*. San Antonio, Texas: The Naylor Company, 1956.

Revis, B.G. "Washington's Two Saddles Gold." *Lost Treasure*. April 1992.

Simmons, Randy. "Treasure of the Sinks." *Lost Treasure*. May 1976.

Wheeler, Jesse H. and J. Trenton Kosbade. *Essentials of World Regional Geography*. Fort Worth, Texas: Harcourt Brace Jovanovich, 1993.